T0246668

JIM LORD

KERRY McDONALD

WITH TRISTAN DAVIES

The author of this book is solely responsible for the accuracy of all facts and statements contained in the book. This is a work of fiction. Names, characters, places, events, and incidents are either the product of the author's imagination or used in an entirely fictitious manner. Any resemblance to actual persons, living or dead, is entirely coincidental.

Copyright © 2023 by Level 4 Press, Inc.

All rights reserved, including the right to reproduce this book, or portions thereof, in any form.

This book is printed on acid-free paper.

Published by:
Level 4 Press, Inc.
14702 Haven Way
Jamul, CA 91935
www.level4press.com

Library of Congress Control Number: 2019943895

ISBN: 978-1-64630-509-4

Printed in the United States of America

Large print edition.

Other books by
KERRY McDONALD

Into Africa
The Green Cathedral

PROLOGUE

Crash and splash.

The atmosphere crushed him. It pressed on his torso like a giant plunger, the weight of its great bell seeking to suck his heart out of his aching chest. He waited for it to seat and complete its bleak chore. But it kept pressing, pressing on his chest, as if controlled from above. It never withdrew.

The memories came in flashes, white bursts of muzzle exhaust in his head. They began benignly enough. A hallway, its linoleum floors polished so they reflected the glare from the bank of fluorescent lights overhead. Red metal lockers with black trim. Doors closed, classes in session.

The smell of floor wax and commercial cleaning solvents. The quiet. Teachers visible through the rectangular windows in the doors. They taught, mouthing their words silently. The students sat at their desks, some listening, others passing notes or surreptitiously checking their phones. Sometimes the teachers turned their backs, scratching on the chalkboards at the front of each room.

Black chalkboards. Walls painted red. Walls spattered red.

His shoes squeaked on the freshly waxed linoleum. He shifted to half-step, smartly, correctly, at attention.

The plunger at his chest tightened its seal.

Outside his motel window, tractor-trailer traffic roared along the interstate. A truck stop was just up the road. The freeway stretched to the marine terminal, the sand pit, and the big

US Steel plant on the pier. The trucks ran all day and all night, the long and loud chug-a-chug of their air brakes boring through Jim Lord's motel room window.

The next muzzle flashes of visions, memories, hallucinations would not let him sleep, no matter how exhausted. The bells rang.

Then came the shouting, insistent, demanding. A radio or walkie-talkie crackled in the spaces between the shouting, filling the silences.

Next came the flashes. The muzzle blasts. Sometimes they blossomed from afar without report. Other times they came from closer in. They came from nearby. They came from very close. They came from beside him.

A face, a bright face edged by a golden halo of hair, floated in the air, smiling at him.

Then a blossoming red.

If Jim did not stand up at that moment, rise from the sagging motel bed, go to the bathroom, and splash water on his face, then burst into the hallway and rush toward the stairwell to find an exit, it would come. The noise would come and then the flash. The noise and the flash came so close to each other that they swallowed him completely.

This one's for you, Bud. Crash and splash. Crash and splash.

1

From the time he could walk, Jim Lord worshipped his namesake, Uncle Jimmy. Maybe it was the uniform. Maybe it was the gun. And maybe it was the car he drove, an old Mustang. Uncle Jimmy, a captain with the Lake County Sheriff's Department, had restored it by himself. Uncle Jimmy wasn't married. Uncle Jimmy liked a good time. And Uncle Jimmy was a hero. Uncle Jimmy was a *cop*.

Like many cops, he was vague about commitment. He liked the ladies. He liked the Majestic Star gambling riverboat docked on Lake Michigan. But every Sunday, without fail,

Uncle Jimmy came for dinner. He took it on himself to be a mentor for his nephew. Uncle Jimmy was a good cop, if of the old school. He wore his prejudices on his sleeve, along with the two gold bars. He was a solid, if not perfect, role model for Jim.

Jim Lord knew before he had known much of anything else that he would become a cop as well. Everyone knew it. None of the Lords doubted it.

Jim was born in the Black Oak section of Gary, Indiana, and raised by his grandparents. He attended Calumet High like his father and mother, even though he'd never really known either. His dad had bailed shortly after he was born, and his mom had died when he wasn't much older. His grandfather had retired from US Steel, and now in the wake of the plant's heyday, Gary was going to hell. But Calumet High remained a decent public high school, despite the changes.

The day after his graduation, Jim applied to the Northwest Indiana Law Enforcement Academy. Uncle Jimmy came through and got the Lake County sheriff to sponsor him. You needed a sponsor. He even got his nephew a partial scholarship.

On the same day, Jim enlisted in the Army Reserve to help pay the other part of his tuition. The only catch was that before he could attend the law enforcement academy, he had to go to basic training.

Jim, who played soccer and ran cross-country at Calumet High, a school that never won anything, spent a hot, aching summer in the Ozarks in basic at Fort Leonard Wood. His records showed him to be a good shot and well above average in strength and stamina. He also received high marks for intellectual potential. He had matured into a robust young man.

When he had completed Advanced Individual Training at Fort Benning, Jim returned to Gary.

However, because he had remained in Georgia for an elective unit in Army intelligence, he missed the January start at the police academy. The intake was only twice a year.

While he waited for the next session, he stayed fit. Each morning he ran a five-mile loop around town. Afternoons he hit the weights at the YMCA in Griffith.

When the police academy started in August, Jim was in the best shape of all the recruits. He was also the best with a weapon, the best with self-defense, and the best with handling a cruiser. He was even the best in keeping his uniform squared away. His time at Fort Benning and Fort Leonard Wood had prepped him well.

The graduation speech was given by the police chief of Valparaiso. An Indiana State Police captain from downstate called out the graduates' names. After the last name was called, most of the graduates threw their hats in the air. Jim didn't. He didn't know how he would find it later.

Later that evening, after Uncle Jimmy's shift had ended, Jim called to thank him. Uncle Jimmy had grown increasingly sullen over the previous few years. There was less gambling and more drinking and yelling at Hannity about the "Blacks" and the "Mexicans."

The fact was, Uncle Jimmy's career had stalled. He blamed it on women in the force and, naturally, minorities. Political correctness, he said, made it impossible for a cop to do his job. He began counting down the days until his twenty came. He said he was going to buy a motorcycle, drive down to Arizona, and stay.

Jim had assumed, incorrectly, that the sponsorship from the Lake County sheriff meant a job would be waiting. There was never a job. And the scholarship program had been shuttered due to nepotism, like the kind Uncle Jimmy had shown his nephew.

"Find a different career," Uncle Jimmy told him over the phone, his words slightly slurred from post-shift drinks. "You don't want this job. It's all Masons and a bunch of porch-sitters from the Westside. You're just not the right constituency, son."

He felt like his uncle had just flushed a toilet and his dreams were circling the bowl. "You should see my rankings from the academy. Pretty high, all of them."

"You don't want this job," Uncle Jimmy repeated. "How about security at the casinos? I know some of those guys up there do pretty good."

"I'm not—" Jim paused. "I want to be a cop, Uncle Jimmy."

Uncle Jimmy never listened too well, which often got him in trouble, even on routine traffic stops.

"I have a buddy from up there, at the Majestic Star, who owns a wrecker company and an impound lot. Does both sides of the line. Does a good business. He's always looking for someone. It can get chippy, towing these night-fighters' cars."

Jim couldn't believe what he was hearing. His mind had been so focused. It had never occurred to him, in his provincial way, that his path was anything but determined.

Jim was nineteen. He had a lot to learn.

Two weeks later, nearly to the day, Jim's cell phone rang.

He almost didn't answer. He'd applied to every single force within a hundred miles. The interest shown was, to be frank, minimal.

Turned out this one was different. On the line was a recruitment officer from the Portage Police Department. Portage was in Porter County, the next county over from Jim's own, Lake.

"Could you come in?" she asked.

And the Portage Police Department hired him. It was a small force. The chief was young and the patrol captain even younger. They were both ex-military. A space had opened when a patrolman had moved to a bigger force. It happened a lot to the smaller police departments.

Portage cops tended not to last long. They moved up and out. As a result, the force was divided between rookies and old-timers who were never going anywhere.

The Quarry Lounge was where the young and more ambitious cops drank. It was Stormy Joe's for the old-timers. Both were dives, and that's the way the cops who drank there liked it.

Probation was six weeks of ride-alongs. There were four turns to a twenty-four-hour period, and Jim worked every shift there was, always changing. He had never been so tired in his life, even at Fort Leonard Wood.

Most units of the Portage patrol were singles,

though there were a few deuces, mainly in Zones 1 and 3, where things could get hairy. Zone 1 was north of the railroad, including both the dunes and the docks. Zone 3, the toughest, was in the northeast quadrant, on the border with Gary.

When Jim passed his probation, he took the only turn that was open. It was the fourth in Zone 4, aka the 4-4, from the Duneland Trail to the south. He patrolled solo. The winter that year was particularly harsh. The only action Jim saw was snow emergencies: stranded drivers, abandoned vehicles, icy skids by a moving vehicle into something unmovable. He bought thermal underwear at Bass Pro and a balaclava. He ordered ski gloves. They came in handy when he had to dig out a car at five a.m.

After Jim had been on the force for eight months, he reached his first period review. Good marks would mean an increase in pay. But the meeting never came.

Before the assigned date, he got an email from the Army Reserve. He was being deployed. Iraq.

Once on base in Iraq, Jim went quickly from signals to SIGINT to straight-up Army intelligence. He didn't speak Arabic, but he had more sense than most about the people who did. There were no questions about his "footing" or "posture." He was all military, all the time. He liked it. The Army liked him.

The intel posting, which was a voluntary lateral promotion, inadvertently caused Jim to increase the time in his tour as a reserve. He did not realize what he had done until it was too late to undo. That wasn't uncommon in the Army. It was standard ops in Intel. He'd be another six months in-country for the privilege of having opted for a more dangerous cadence. Brilliant.

He was stationed forward at a small firebase out of which ran most of his ops. He was assigned to a crew of about thirty men, all from mixed backgrounds—regular Army, naval intel, a couple Marines, special forces, CIA field officers, and even two FBI agents. It was completely off-book. Just the existence of such a magpie group of services working together was, quite literally, illegal. Jim was a signals officer. As such he was responsible for parsing the missions they received, which were complex and even contradictory, basically making the egg back out of the scramble.

Which isn't to say he didn't ride along. He did. A lot of the time. Because he was the pencil-neck, the egghead, he didn't ride in the van, but with an outfit that small, he was never far from the kinetics when they occurred. Jim saw stuff. Jim did stuff. War you don't talk about. Secret wars you don't even think about.

Jim told the CO what he best thought the operation was. The CO told the staff lieutenant. The unit moved most often in three Black Hawks. When the three ships reached the beach, the men in the first two to land would figure out if the mission-meet had anything to do with reality.

Sometimes it did. Sometimes it didn't. And sometimes it was a real hot mess. Jim had ridden on all three.

Thankfully, he only flew one mission the whole time in-country that was a complete dog's breakfast, dust-off to dust-down. That was the trip they lost two of their own. Two stars on the wall. Or maybe not. Who knew, in the end.

At the forward base, officers from the different ops bivouacked together. The first friend Jim made was a blue-eyed and kind-hearted guy named Kevin Gallagher. K-Tell, as he was called, came from Roxbury, Mass., which was a little like Jim being from Gary. He was Navy, on loan to another secret operations group. Sometimes he talked too fast for Jim to understand what he was saying. Jim and K-Tell never spoke about their individual missions. That was just the way it was.

Over the first few weeks on base, however, they shared a lot of other things. Military friendship is a shy and territorial thing. It resembles a high school clique, organized crime membership, or the indescribable devotion of a religious order. They spent most of their non-duty time together. They were a "team," in other words, the basic unit of combat organization. The root of the fighting machine.

The officers' bivy sat next to the medic tent. At any time, day or night, the quiet of the desert might be punctuated by the rising *thock-thock-thock* of an incoming medical flight. Sometimes, when there was more than one chopper, an orderly would appear at the flap of the bivy and yell for men to help hump the incoming racks into the medic tent. That was the worst action Jim saw on his tour, casualty-wise, what came in on the Black Hawks—men, hardly recognizable, who had burned through both their morphine pops plus whatever it was they got on the flight and were screaming still.

One afternoon, Jim was in his crib doing an old crossword left behind by one of the flights from Germany. At first, the noise could have been normal traffic. But it kept getting louder, closer, the sure sign that medevacs were incoming. And then the *thock-thock-thock* got louder still. There was more than one of them out there, loitering above the tents, awaiting their turn to land.

A particularly distressed call came from an orderly at the flap of Jim's bivy, barking harder than Jim had ever heard. There was a red ball express coming in. The *git* was about to *hit*.

Jim jumped into his boots and pulled on

his gloves. He reached the pad just as the first Black Hawk was negotiating its footing. Both bays were full: eight wounded. At least two more choppers dangled out in the bright afternoon sun.

Jim waited in the line of volunteers being pelted by the dust and debris swirling in the wash kicked up by the rotors. His turn came with the last rack off the first Black Hawk. He grabbed the two handles on his end of the litter just as the medic inside the bay unclipped the carabiners holding it fast. The men in the chopper were jacked and shouting, even over their headsets. Jim's partner took the forward duty and they barely had the stretcher free before the rotors powered up again and the skids lifted off the dirt.

Because Jim had the back grips, he could see the soldier in the litter, wrapped unevenly in shining yellow body insulation. The man had been thrashing in pain and the stretcher was smeared with a heavy coating of blood mixed with dirt. His eyes were big as saucers, perfectly round and white, contorted by shock. He looked as close to death as possible while still alive.

Then he was sucked inside the triage tent flap by a pair of medics.

Jim raced back to the landing zone and again waited in line. The litters bounced by, their high-denier mesh sagging with the bodies of the wounded. The scene was awash with blood. It covered the hands and clothes of the volunteers. It ran down the sides of the Black Hawks, spurting onto the yellow pancake dirt of the LZ, and it mixed so thoroughly with everything that Jim could taste it, along with the dirt and kerosene exhaust, in his parched mouth.

He took the next to last litter off the last of the Black Hawks that had been loitering. Again, he got the back grips. As the onboard medic unclipped the rack, Jim looked again into the face of the wounded. It was a guy he recognized, one of the Navy loans pulling ops duty as a sapper for K-Tell's unit. He was conscious and responsive. The last of the medevacs flew the least serious of the casualties.

"What went down?" Jim asked.

"Fubar," the wounded man said. "From the second we inserted. Total, complete disaster."

"Was K-Tell riding?"

Considering the bullet lodged in his shoulder, the man's look of sympathy at the question was unnerving.

"K-Tell was riding in the van, man."

Back in his tent, Jim stared for two hours at his recycled crossword without filling in a single square. Finally, he got his courage up to where he could drift over to the post-op tent. Men stood around the bunks with friends or company mates. It looked as if every bunk was

full. There wasn't a man or woman there without a rack and a drip, or even two. Two patients
rode vents. It was bad.

Jim walked up and down the bunks twice
before he looked for someone to ask. Finally,
he found an exhausted nurse with dried blood
all over his surgical smock and sleeves.

"One of the guys on the last Black Hawk told
me that K-Tell Gallagher came in. You see him?"

"Sure." That was it. The man was bone-weary.

"Is he around?" Jim asked. "I took a pass
through the recovery tent but no dice."

"Dude," the nurse said, "he came in on the
first Black Hawk. In the front flap and out the
back. They turned him right around to Bagram.
He's probably halfway to Germany by now."

"Was it bad?"

"It wasn't good. I mean, look at these people.
These are the ones we *kept*. But he's in the limo
now. They'll throw whatever they've got at him."

Jim would never hear whether K-Tell lived

or died. That was just the way it went in intelligence. They didn't exist in-country in the first place; how could they die? Kevin Gallagher— they didn't even exchange email addresses or APOs or FPOs. Like all twenty-year-olds, they figured they would live forever. There'd be time for that grandpa, Christmas-card crap later.

At the end of Jim's extended tour, the Army asked him for more. He had just gotten back in-country from five days in Frankfurt drinking beer and wandering around the old city. He might have gone on to Baltimore and found a way to get to Gary, but he didn't. He might have taken a knee and not taken rest and recuperation time at all. He was close enough to being sent home.

In some strange way, he thought he might bump into K-Tell on a street somewhere. The closest he got was a friendly Irish girl humming along to some jazz in a small bar near the hostel where he stayed. She had deep blue eyes and umber hair that smelled of expensive shampoo. "Dark Irish," she told him. They ate sausage and drank beer at an outside table at the Chicken Market. She took him to a jazz club. He bought her a pack of cigarettes, withholding one as tax. They spent the whole night walking around town. After a coffee at dawn, she was on a bus to the airport. Back to Dublin.

The colonel who was the ranking officer in Jim's unit sat him down on his return.

"I'm talking about going up the hawser hole," he said, using Navy slang for getting promoted to officer status out of the enlisted ranks.

"Time off for a spell at OTS, which is like a walk in the country compared with this stuff." He waved. "This is a forever war, Jim. And you're good. You're good at what you do. You're good in the unit. The Army could do good things for you. And we, us, the other guys, we need you now, here, with us."

Jim thanked his CO and asked leave to think about it.

"You don't need to ask, Jim," he said. "Just say yes when you can."

But Jim already knew what his answer would be. He hadn't seen anything nearly as bad as he had the day K-Tell got hit. In fact, he'd only been outside the wire a handful of times since. Things had quieted down. The action was farther east. Jim knew that if he re-upped, sooner or later they'd get the word to stuff their sacks and be ready to re-deploy. There was already chatter about ops running along the Iranian border. Hairy stuff.

Jim was not afraid. For himself, at least. But he was done with the *thock-thock-thock*, done with the taste of blood and dirt. Iraqi dirt. American blood. He had seen enough.

Jim wanted to return to Indiana and get back to being a cop. Like Uncle Jimmy.

He gave the CO his answer and got a butt-chewing in return. He spent a night at Bagram. At Ramstein he changed planes at two a.m.

The return to Gary, quick and painless, was anticlimactic.

Jim didn't call on the Portage department for two days after he got back. He felt he deserved at least that. And it gave him time to find his own place. He was too old to live with his grandparents, so he took a small one-bedroom. It came with used furniture and dishes, and that suited him just fine. He didn't know how to decorate and didn't care to learn.

Once he was situated, he went to the department. The duty sergeant was named Dabchick. Dabchick hated Commies and Muslims and Europeans, particularly the French. He had an American flag decal on the window of his Cutlass. But for some reason, he didn't much respect military service. He thought being a cop was more patriotic than being in the Army any day.

They had only traded hellos before Dabchick dropped the bad news. "Things are pretty tight these days."

"There's a job for me, Sarge. I know that. It's the law. I was in Iraq. The war? Army Reserve?"

"I know what the law is, son." Dabchick kept looking down at his blotter. There was nothing there; the schedule was online. That was how Jim knew it was bad. "Maybe you've been away, but we've been having tough times here. You read the papers? You look around town? Things is tough right now. Everybody's struggling. You're no special case, son."

"Yes, sir," Jim replied. His guts churned. Jim had served his country.

"Don't crap yourself, officer," Dabchick said finally. "You got a job. I just got to figure where to put you."

The next few days were tough. Jim didn't have anyone to talk to. He couldn't trouble his grandparents. They were too old for his dramas. And Uncle Jimmy was more and more out of touch with reality.

On Thursday the civilian secretary called him. Jim expected the worst.

"Hey, Jim?" she began. "How was the war?"

"Bloody," he said. "Loud."

"I bet. War is hell, right? Anyway, be here first turn tomorrow. Patrol uniform."

Jim went to a nearby tavern. He drank two celebratory beers at the bar and ate an enchilada plate.

He was a cop again.

***

The next morning, before reporting to the station, Jim stopped at a doughnut shop across the street from Calumet, his old school. He'd gone there nearly every day before his deployment; they had even known his usual, an iced coffee.

Jim recognized the owner, an Indian guy, was still there and getting the shop started. The owner didn't recognize him, beyond his being a cop, to which he nodded as he carried a flat of doughnuts to the back to be baked.

Even with that stop, Jim got to the station early. He found an empty locker and stashed his bag in it, putting on his own lock. He went to the cage and got his ammunition and the rest of the gear for his duty belt: radio, baton, handcuffs, pepper spray.

"You're not on for a vest," said the registrar, a newbie.

"No vest?" Jim asked. "What's up with that?"

The kid looked again at the roster sheet for the first turn.

"No vest. No long gun," he said. Regular patrolmen were issued a shotgun for each turn.

The truth of the matter was revealed at the morning briefing: Jim was on school resource officer duty at Portage High School.

He closed his eyes in disbelief.

SRO was the job that went to incompetent cops either protected by the union or on their way out of the system. SRO was the aspiration of natural resource cops who wanted out of the cold and the wind. SRO was the deadest dead end. SRO was babysitting.

Jim pulled into the parking lot at Portage High in a daze. The first person he met inside was the bubbly school office administrator, Patti Triplett, who appeared to be only a little older than himself. Even in the dead of Indiana

winter she sported a deep tan, and her finger-
nails were impeccably painted. Bright pink,
just like her sweater set.

"How lucky your first day is a Friday," she
chirped. "One day and then the weekend!"

Next, a pimply member of the Blue Key
Honor Society gave him a tour of the campus.
Jim did not pay close attention. He still couldn't
believe his assignment was real.

When they returned to the admin suite,
Patti introduced him to the other SRO. Tom
Harbaugh was a big Central Indiana guy who
had become an SRO after working for none other than the Department of Natural Resources.

"It's great!" Tom said after standing to greet
him. His big frame nearly filled the small office
they were to share, which Jim figured had to
have once been a janitorial closet, right next
door to the admin suite.

He's fresh off pulling illegal badger traps,
Jim thought.

Tom wore the SRO uniform, a black polo with a silver star embossed on the breast and an undershirt beneath. It was meant to be less threatening to the students than a regular uniform.

"The good news is," Tom said, "last bell is at 2:35. The last bus usually pulls out no later than 3:15. And you're outta here!"

After the last school bus left the parking lot, Jim drove to the station and checked his gear. From the station he drove to the Quarry Lounge.

He got a couple of backslaps and even a "Thank you for your service" or two from the cops there who recognized him. He hated it as much as any other person who ever served did. By his second beer, Jim had laid it all out.

"I mean, what do I do?" he asked. "Who's the, I don't know, union rep or whatever?"

An old-timer, a real bull, a professional private, sitting farther down the bar drinking his inevitable mug of beer, laughed. "You got dinged with babysitting?"

"What's up with that?" Jim called down to him, thankful for the commiseration. "I thought I was supposed to get my job back. I thought that was the law."

"You did get your job back," the older cop said. "It's called babysitting. Crash and splash." And with those words he burst into a fit of laughter, and the guys around him joined in. Babysitting sucked, and everybody knew it.

Crash and splash? Jim thought. *What the heck?*

"What did I do?" he pushed. "I mean, is there some talk about me?"

"Nah," said one of the cops Jim had been friendly with before he deployed. "It's the 'collapse' or whatever they call it. The stuff with the banks. You just got home at the wrong time."

Jim spent the weekend angry. The humiliation burned inside him. He remembered what he had thought of the school cop when he was at Calumet. Everybody knew that a school cop was a failed cop.

That weekend Jim met his Uncle Jimmy for lunch at the Bull and Bear, a dark singles hangout over near Jimmy's apartment building. Jimmy insisted his nephew order a rack of baby back ribs, the house specialty.

Uncle Jimmy had become only more bitter about his life. He cast blame aplenty: mouthy minorities, tight-assed femi-nazis, and millennials—the usual suspects. Jim was surprised Uncle Jimmy didn't mention black helicopters; that was how far out he had gotten on the Hannity thing.

Uncle Jimmy tore into his third moisturized towelette and wiped his mouth. An impressive array of sucked-clean bones lay piled on his platter.

"How was Iraq?" he asked, but Jim knew he was just asking to be polite. Jimmy thought Iraq was a fake war set up by the bankers and those types. Besides, his eyes were on the clock by the bar, and Jim figured he was probably thinking about the date he'd mentioned having with a woman he met at Pastore's, a meat market for the over-forty set.

"Good enough," Jim said. "I saw a lot."

Uncle Jimmy smiled, as if he knew what Jim was talking about.

"There's a lot of talk about how it was actually the English and not the Russians who poisoned that spy."

"Listen, Uncle Jimmy," Jim said, redirecting the conversation. "I'm back now at my job. But they put me on SRO."

Uncle Jimmy perked up. "That's bull," he said. "SRO?"

"What should I do?"

Jimmy leaned back in his chair and thought about it for a moment.

"You're done, kid," he said. "That's the sad truth about it. Find yourself something new to do. I hear you can make real money fracking over in Ohio."

2

On Monday, Jim got better acquainted with the school's building. Portage High was designed like a ladder, with two long hallways running parallel to each other. These north and south halls, painted yellow and lined with red lockers, intersected with three shorter passages, the A, B, and C halls, where the activity spaces were located: the theater, the industrial arts shop, and the music rooms. The cafeteria was housed at the west end where the hallways met, with the administration suite tucked in the corner beside it.

On the east end, the main entrance to the school featured a large lobby surrounded by benches, where the athletes and popular students gravitated. The doors opened onto the Skirt, a paved area with a flag and a terrible and anachronistic bronze sculpture of Shabbona, a Potawatomi warrior. He had supposedly fought bravely during the Beaver Wars. The Portage High teams were still called the Indians.

As Jim swept down the south hallway looking for stragglers to class, he passed a teacher conversing with a student outside her classroom. The teacher was tall and slim and dark, with a red silk scarf draped over her shoulders and jeans that mostly hid a pair of brown boots, one of which was propping the classroom door open just a crack.

Jim glanced through the door's window to see a chemistry lab, which was appropriate given their location. English and social studies each occupied half of the north hallway. Math and science shared the south.

As she listened to the girl, whose blond

ponytail swished side to side as she talked animatedly, the teacher's eyes flicked to Jim, and she met his gaze. He blushed and looked down, picking up his tempo if only inadvertently. She was pretty.

Jim got to Portage High early the next morning. He wanted time to explore the place and understand it without teenagers churning around.

He walked the science section of the south hallway first, then the other half where the math classes were held. Jim had been quite good at math at Calumet High. But the math kids were geeks, even worse than the computer weirdos, because at least the computer freaks could play mean Doom. When Jim got placed in calculus, none of his friends were and he felt ashamed. He took elective shop instead.

In the east lobby he paused. At the center of the space a brass school seal was inset in the floor. Once it had been protected by stan-chions and ropes, presumably. Now only the bolt marks in the tile remained. The seal was well and regularly trod on.

"Just wait until graduation," Tom Harbaugh had told him on his first day, nodding at the seal. "You'll see."

Another amateurish rendition of Shabbona took up almost the entirety of the south wall, a caricature of the savage Indian warrior. Indians had lived all through that part of Indiana. The state was even named for them: *Indiana*. There were barrows and mounds all over the place. The Indiana Indians had fought back until nearly the Civil War before all getting killed or marched off to Kansas or Oklahoma.

"Which unit?"

The voice from behind startled Jim, who had seen only a worker servicing the vending machines outside the cafeteria when he began his sweep.

He turned to see a man with sandy-blond hair and reading glasses low on his nose holding an attendance notebook in an open classroom doorway. Jim couldn't tell his age. He was neatly dressed and fit, and he could have been anywhere from thirty-five to fifty-five. His faced was tanned like that of a man who had spent much of the summer out of doors. His posture had a sense of readiness.

"I'm sorry, sir?" Jim said.

"I said which unit, soldier. As in, what's your unit, buddy?"

"Oh," Jim replied, startled by the teasing familiarity. "I was—Wait. Sorry. Is it that obvious?"

"No, really?" The man grinned.

"National Guard," Jim said.

"Unit?"

"Seventy-sixty," Jim said. Civilians liked to act as if they were cognizant. Naming the combat team usually put an end to their knowing questions.

"Black Hawks," the man said.

"How did you know that?" Jim offered his hand and the man considered it before reciprocating.

"I'm Marlow. Chuck Marlow. How long were you deployed?"

Again, Jim wondered how it was so obvious. His hair had grown out and been cut. Already he could tell he had softened and stiffened a bit from when he was at his fighting weight. "I did a year in Iraq," he said.

"Full stretch," Marlow said.

"When I got there, I switched into SIGINT. That earned me some extra time. They like to keep the intel guys around longer. You serve, I guess?"

"Navy," Marlow said.

Jim wondered if the tone in his voice was wistful. "You do a tour?" Still unable to place his age, he couldn't do the math familiar to any veteran—given the person's age, calculating instantly what war it was they had fought, or avoided.

"I was Navy Special WARCOM," Marlow said.

Special Warfare, Jim thought. Different from SEALs. Spooks. Ghosts in the field.

"I fought my war in Central America," Marlow added. "The Northern Triangle."

"Dope," Jim said. "Sandinistas and Zapatistas?"

"Sure. And Sendero Luminoso and cartels. A lot of cartels."

"Are you still serving reserves?" Jim asked.

Marlow smiled beneath his glasses. "Old soldiers, as the saying goes."

"Sure," Jim said. "Never die."

Jim carried on toward the administrative offices and the cafeteria. At least there was another vet on staff at Portage. That had to be a good thing.

A student in a Portage cheer uniform affixed office-approved posters to an announcement board that ran the length of one wall in the west lobby. Jim was pretty sure it was the same girl he'd seen talking to the chemistry teacher the day before. She was tall and slim and blond with glossy waxed legs that ran from her ridiculously flounced—and short—cheer skirt down to her red and white saddle shoes. Jim wondered if adolescent girls anywhere else in the world were objectified in that kind of display. Certainly not in Iraq. He knew that much.

"You're the new SRO," she said. In one hand she held a fistful of yellow sheets announcing a spay and neuter program. In the other she held an office stapler, cocked open. The heel of her right palm was reddened by the repeated pounding.

"Hi," Jim said lamely. He didn't know what the protocol was on addressing a student.

"I'm Amber." She clamped the open stapler in her left armpit and stuck out a hand in a deliberate motion, like a chop. "Amber Parker."

"Hi, Amber." He wanted her to tell him how the students were supposed to address their SROs. Was he Officer Lord? That sounded stupid.

She smiled conspiratorially and leaned so close he could smell the fruit of her shampoo. "Jim," she said in an almost whisper.

Jim took an uncomfortable step back, remembering after a panicky moment the name-plate above his badge. *Okay, so that's settled.* At least for Amber Parker.

"You a big pet person?" he asked, nodding at the poster she'd just hung.

"Love 'em." Amber put her hands on her hips and struck an admonishing pose. *"Just not their unwanted and uncared for pups and kittens."*

Jim looked more carefully at the poster. The phrase came verbatim from the Comic Sans text that danced below sketches of a kitty and puppy frolicking together.

"It's a service project," Amber said. "Gotta get those service hours."

"Good cause. Animal welfare."

"Sure. If you're an animal control officer."

That stung. Jim knew that in addition to natural resource officers like Tom Harbaugh, animal control officers—*dog catchers*—often landed SRO duty.

"I'm a Portage Police officer," Jim bleated, despite himself. He felt immediately embarrassed.

Amber flashed a straight-A student grin. "Of course. *Officer* Jim."

"Right, okay," Jim said. "Listen. I'm glad to meet you, Amber."

"See you at the student council meeting on Thursday. I'm president." She winked before striding out of the lobby. Not an entirely innocent wink, either, he didn't think.

Jim sighed in exasperation. *Crash and splash, all right*, he thought.

***

On fifth period sweep, Jim started again at the science hallway. To his nervous surprise, the chemistry teacher with the dark updo, now wearing nerdy librarian glasses and black stockings, stood outside her empty classroom. Jim guessed she was a few years older than he was, but probably still in her mid-twenties. She taped a *Scientific American* article to the wall just outside her door. *Postering happens a lot at Portage High*, Jim thought.

He stopped a few paces off, intending to say something but instead finding himself dumb.

"Hello?" she said, noticing him hovering. When he failed to reply, she added, "Do you speak?"

Her sarcasm caught him off guard.

"Hi," Jim managed to say. "Jim." He gestured to his nameplate.

"Amber Parker thinks you're cute," the woman said. "I hope you don't feel reciprocally?"

"Reciprocally?"

"Yes, reciprocally. I'm a chemistry teacher, remember?"

"Yes." Jim flushed and fumbled for words. "I mean, no. I mean . . . yes, I know what reciprocally means and, no, I don't feel that way toward Amber Parker."

"But do you know what the law of reciprocal proportions is and who Jeremiah Richter was?"

Jim panicked, thinking he should have gone to college.

"I'm Malinda," she said with a smirk. "Murch. Though I don't have a—" She nodded toward Jim's nameplate.

"Badge?" he said.

"'We don't need no stinking badges,'" she said with a mock accent.

This one, at least, Jim understood, and he chuckled. "Gosh, no."

"Gosh?" An eyebrow shot up and she raised her glasses to her forehead.

"What I mean is"—Jim took a deep breath to calm his rattled nerves—"I met Amber Parker earlier today. She's quite a . . . a . . ."

"Specimen, do you mean to say?" Malinda's tone made it clear she was teasing.

"That's biology," Jim countered, finally regaining his command of speech. "I thought you taught chemistry."

"Ah, touché, officer. An emulsion, then?"

"And not an aerosol?"

"Say, you're quite the scholar, Officer Lord."

"I had a good chemistry teacher."

"Good as me?" Malinda smiled coyly.

"Probably not," Jim said with his own shy smile.

* * *

On the Skirt that afternoon, Jim and Tom Harbaugh stood talking as they supervised the first dismissal, for upperclassmen.

"I should fill you in," Tom said, "on some pranks going on."

"Pranks?" So much of this was both new and, from a different perspective, familiar from his days not so long ago at Calumet High.

"This one is real borderline," Tom said. "I'm okay with the juvenile stuff, the letting off steam stuff. We all did it. I get it. This one is a little off."

"What's the drill?"

"Small explosions. They go off in the parking lot. So far, it's been during classes with nobody around. At first, it was just small stuff. Nothing bigger than a firecracker. Moved to cherry bomb. I found plenty of scorch marks. Maybe some kid had been to Pennsylvania and brought back a butt-load of them. But they keep getting bigger. A junior had to go to the nurse last week after lunch because she temporarily lost hearing in one ear."

Jim suddenly heard the deafening *thock-thock-thock* the Black Hawks made when they circled the pads and landed outside the medic tent.

"What's the point?" he asked.

"At first, like I said, just pranking. Getting ready for the senior week in the spring," Tom said. "Some of these guys are real country boys. You'd be surprised how fast it gets real downstate at the end of the year."

Downstate meant rural. Farmland. Soy and corn.

"But it's only January. And setting off explosives in the parking lot?"

Tom just shook his head. "Let me tell you, it can get pretty crazy."

"Are there targets? Do they single anybody out?"

"Dorks, typically. The nerds seem to get it. Dorks and pretty girls."

After finishing his second-bell sweep for third period the next day, Jim dropped by Chuck Marlow's classroom. Before knocking, he surveyed the indifference and subsequent chaos in the room. Whereas many of the other teachers carefully covered the walls with colorful instructional materials, Marlow had only a large Mercator map of the world pinned to one wall. The other walls were bare. Rather than assigned desks in orderly ranks, Marlow had sourced folding rectangular tables, arranged in a square with a large space for him to wander in when he lectured. The kids sat wherever they pleased.

Despite Jim's short tenure at the school, he'd already heard Marlow chastise a student for sitting in the same spot. "'Consistency is the hobgoblin of little minds,'" he had heard him say through the open door, making the student move to a different place around the square. But the unorthodoxy apparently had a method. When Jim had peered in a while later, the pupils seemed fully attentive. Rapt, one might even say. Patti Triplett had told him Marlow was consistently the most popular instructor in the school. As well as the bane of the administration for his unconventional methods.

Jim rapped on the door when Marlow didn't look up, his nose in a stack of papers. The history teacher had an off period, and Jim found him seated at one of the students' tables, which was pushed into a corner and covered with newspapers and magazines.

"Jim, it's you," Marlow said, glancing up. "Come in." He gestured to the empty room while his eyes returned to the paper he was grading. He gripped a red pen and jotted something in the margin.

"You stay involved at all?" Jim asked, stepping

inside. "Groups, VFW, the OCS Alum group? Any of that?"

"I fly," Marlow said, his pen shooting across the paper as he either underlined or crossed something out.

"Fly?" Jim asked.

"I flew Orions out of Whidbey Island. For a while at least. For some reason I was a savant in the T-34s we used for training. I could just fly the hell out of those things. That's why I got sent to Venezuela." He pronounced it in an exaggerated singsong: *Ven-eh-zoo-ehh-la.*

So, Marlow was both Naval Special WARCOM and an aviator. The story kept getting more interesting.

"Do you know about these school bombings?" Jim asked.

"You mean the hijinks in the parking lot? Now it's *bombing*?" Marlow set the pen down. He took a red bandanna from his hip pocket and wiped his glasses. It was an interesting touch, given the overall preppy aspect of Marlow's clothes otherwise.

"Yes," Jim said. "That stuff."

"Let's have lunch together. Get this nonsense out of your system." Marlow pulled a black-vinyl datebook from beneath the unruly pile of papers he was working through.

What surprised Jim then, given the casual nature of the way Marlow ran things, was the absolute order in his daybook. The pages were written in a fastidious hand, the margins filled with further meticulous entries and addenda. Page after page had course notes, reading records, lecture ideas, and lists of student meetings, all in the same remarkably tidy and unrushed penmanship. Open lunch dates, of which there were few, were marked with a triple hash mark. Marlow found one the following week.

"Does that work?" he asked, virtually rhetorically, pointing at the date. "Meet me here after your sweeps."

Jim next glimpsed Malinda Murch between second and third periods the following morning.

The chemistry teacher was in the hallway just after second bells, when the doors should have been closed and class sessions begun. Her hair was swept up in a messy bun, and a pair of safety glasses perched insouciantly on her brow, like sunglasses. She was talking again to Amber Parker, who looked every bit the student body vice president in a chocolate corduroy skirt and a cappuccino mohair sweater.

"I know it's him," Amber said. "It's just got to be. It all adds up. Who else in this place—let's face it—is smart enough?"

"Mr. Lord," Malinda said as she noticed Jim

approach. Jim thought he saw the hint of a smile in her eyes, brown and very clear.

"Oh, hi, Jim. What's jumping?" Then Amber's face lit up and she waved her arm toward him. "Actually, he should know. Except he probably doesn't, since he just got here." She faced Jim triumphantly. "I think we have a prime suspect for the bombings."

"A suspect?" Jim said.

"Absolutely. A male, of course, due to the misogynistic terror inflicted by the perpetrator."

"Oh, Amber." Malinda pinched the bridge of her nose with two fingers, as if warding off a migraine.

"Karsten Nygard," Amber continued, unfazed. "The Brigand from Brigata Hills."

"Where do you come up with this stuff?" Malinda lamented.

"What? That's where he lives. That nice development down off 550. His dad is an engineer from Purdue who invented some squiggly thing that goes in nuclear warheads."

"Why do they live all the way up here, then?" Malinda asked.

"I think the mom does research in Michigan City at the GM Works. The one that develops the *explosives in air bags*?"

"Okay, okay," Malinda said. "I think that's enough. Go. Get." She pulled open the door, which she had propped open with one brown boot, a different pair from the one Jim had noticed before, this one more of an English riding style.

"Let's talk more about it when you're not in class," Jim said.

Amber shrugged and, books clutched to her chest, bounced into the lab.

"Are you asking her out or me?" Malinda asked, still holding the door.

"You," Jim said quickly. "Clearly you."

Malinda nodded and then turned to follow Amber. As she closed the door behind her, she flashed Jim a sly grin through the window.

Maybe crashing and splashing isn't so bad after all, he thought.

After eighth period, Jim met Tom Harbaugh out on the Skirt to supervise the first round of departures.

"Is it ever going to get cold this winter?" Tom asked. He wore only a light jacket over his short-sleeved SRO performance-wear polo. Jim had on his down service jacket and still struggled to get warm. Tom was an outdoorsy type. To him, cold meant a long enough and hard enough freeze to be able to go ice fishing on Pine Lake over in La Porte.

Amber Parker appeared before them, dressed now in a Portage High warmup jacket and black leggings. She was headed in the direction of the field house, across the playing fields beyond the student parking lot.

"Jim," she said. "Long time no."

"Where you headed?" Jim asked. "Don't you have student council today?"

"That's old news, Jim. Met at lunch." She shifted her heavy backpack from one shoulder to the other. "Now it's cheerleading practice. Captain, if you're interested. Basketball game tomorrow. You should come watch." She popped a flex with her left bicep. "Indiana strong!" she called as she sauntered off.

"She has never once called me by my name," Tom said when she was out of earshot. "You stud, Lord. Look at you."

"Is there anything that girl doesn't do?"

"I wish I knew," Tom said wistfully, and Jim wondered if Tom realized the question had been ironic. "Did you know she's varsity volleyball in the fall and runs hurdles for track in the spring?" Tom's gaze followed her progress toward the field house. "Her flexibility is amazing."

Jim couldn't tell if Tom was just impressed by her athleticism or his mind was going elsewhere, so he steered the conversation to a safer topic. "Back to the firecrackers or explosions or whatever. Any suspects?"

"Nah," Tom said, bringing his focus back to Jim. "I mean, there's maybe one. It's this kid, Karsten Nygard. Kind of a strange kid. Loner. Keeps to himself. You know, prime suspect for a postal shooting. But the kid is so out of it, I don't know. I think he's just a dork. Believe it or not, I was pretty dorky as a kid, too."

"No way, Tom." His sarcasm was again lost on its recipient. Tom Harbaugh, despite his lumberjack beard and outdoorsy build, was as big a dork as they came. "Not you."

"Yup. Kind of heavy. Into D&D. That stuff. Funny dice."

"Never would have guessed," Jim said. "If you hadn't told me."

"Some kids just mature late. I knew this guy in high school. I mean, if you saw him now—"

A burst of what sounded like small-caliber fire popped from the parking lot beyond the Skirt. A scream quickly followed, and Jim's mind flashed to Amber.

Tom ran left down one aisle of cars, and Jim split right down the next.

On the far periphery of the lot, students had gathered, and more came running toward the commotion. When Jim raced up, he found them gawping at a tricked-out white Ford F-150 with a jacked-up chassis and a glossy white bed cover. A big kid in a sweatshirt with the sleeves ripped off and rocking a thick gold chain around his far thicker neck stood behind the tailgate looking disoriented. Jim and Tom reached him at about the same time, and each took an arm.

"Are you hurt?" Tom asked.

"No," the kid said dully, shaking his buzz-cut head. "No, nope. I'm not." But he looked a little dazed and he talked fast and too loudly. Jim recognized him as Kevin White, a football player and wrestler. He fit the lunkhead jock cliché closely.

A wide circle of black soot was burned into the faded asphalt near the driver-side door. In the air hung a smell Jim remembered from launching Estes model rockets as a kid. Kevin blinked a few times, appearing to come back to his senses.

"What the hell?" he cried. "Look at my truck!" A band of black soot ran vertically up the driver-side door. "I mean, what the . . ." He trailed off in a primal growl.

"Language, White," Jim said. "It looks mostly okay. No structural damage."

"'Mostly okay'?" Kevin, still a bit deaf,

bellowed. "It's got a big ugly black thing on it! That thing. It's a . . ."

"White," Tom cautioned, before turning his attention to the gathering of students. "Hey! That's all. Show's over. Go home. Scoot."

Reluctantly, the curious peeled off in ones and twos.

"I swear to God!" Kevin fumed, pacing beside his truck. "When I find out who did this, I'll effin' kill him."

"Language, Kevin," Tom said, sighing. "Nobody is killing anybody."

"Where were you when it detonated?" Jim asked.

"What?"

"When it blew up," Tom supplied.

"I know what detonated means," White retorted angrily. "About where you are, I guess." He pointed toward Jim. "I was coming to get my wrestling gear out of my truck."

"See anything suspicious?" Jim asked. "Wires, a package, anything like that?"

"No, nothing. I was looking at my phone anyway. Then, *bang!*" he shouted, throwing out his arms and nearly clobbering Tom. "I could have got hurt!"

"Okay, okay," Jim said. "Unlock it and I'll get your wrestling bag."

Kevin beeped the truck lock, and Jim pulled open the passenger-side door. Briefly it occurred to him that there might be more to come, if someone had targeted Kevin White specifically, but his instincts told him otherwise.

He grabbed the duffel and tossed it to the stocky kid in the sweatshirt.

"We'll keep the keys," Tom said. "You can pick them up in the office after wrestling practice."

"No effin' way! What are you going to do to my truck?"

"White!" Tom barked. Then in a calmer tone,

"We're going to look it over and make sure it's safe. Get to practice."

With a defiant shake of his head, Kevin turned and stalked off toward the field house.

"What do you think?" Tom asked Jim.

Jim knelt and looked under the truck. "There isn't anything here. Either it was a simple device, or it was strong enough to blow itself apart. This is fairly sophisticated kinetics."

"Not just a cherry bomb or M-80 or whatever?"

"Not a cherry bomb," Jim said. "Way more than a cherry bomb."

Tom and Jim inspected the truck, taking the opportunity to also check for alcohol, weapons, and drugs. There were some bottle caps on the floor of the crew cab and a disposable e-cigarette in one of the seat pouches, but nothing else.

No sign of what had caused the explosion, or who was behind it.

*** *

Blackbird Café was a coffeehouse down in Valparaiso that catered to the artsy students on the Valparaiso U. campus. Malinda Murch walked through the door shortly after Jim arrived. The coffee had been Jim's idea. The café had been Malinda's. It featured rough-hewn wooden tables and exposed-brick walls. Loopy Indian music played in the background.

"I live in Valparaiso," she explained once they were ensconced in a corner table, "because it's more interesting than Portage, frankly."

Jim just shrugged. Malinda ordered a cortado with soy milk. Jim ordered a cortado with regular milk, not actually knowing what a cortado was. It turned out to be a *glass* of coffee, and not a big one, either.

Malinda taught intro chemistry and AP chemistry. As it turned out, she was not a Hoosier at all. She had grown up in Pittsburgh and studied chemical engineering at Carnegie Mellon.

When the conversation petered out organically, Jim decided to broach the subject of school. "What's the deal with this kid Amber Parker was talking about? Karsten Nygard?"

"You seem awfully chummy with Amber Parker," Malinda said.

Jim couldn't tell if she was joking. If she was, she had a good poker face.

"Just doing my job, ma'am," he said.

"You'd recognize him if I pointed him out," she said. "He's a real SLK."

Jim tipped his head, trying to process the letters. The K through 12 education system had nearly as many acronyms as policing and the military. Jim was trying to get on top of the jargon, and "SLK" was one he hadn't heard yet.

"*Strange-looking kid,*" Malinda clarified. "You use it for a kid who just doesn't look right. As a teacher you pick up on it right away. Acts weird, dresses weird, doesn't fit in with the other kids."

"So scientific."

Malinda laughed. She was prettier even than Jim had thought before. She carried herself with a natural poise.

"Maybe the kid is on the spectrum," she continued. "Maybe a violent home. Maybe it's abuse. Whatever it is, it shows itself. Sometimes enough that you've got to make a referral."

"A referral for what?"

"For being an SLK!" Malinda said. They both laughed. "He's definitely a bright kid. But the things he's interested in—model rockets. Jet propellants. He brought me an article from a science journal he found online about ZIFs."

"Uh, again? ZIFs?"

"Zeolitic imidazolate frameworks. I learned about them in college. Basically, it's space-age solid rocket fuel. I mean, crazy stuff. The kind of stuff that's going to send a man to Mars. Super potent stuff."

"Explosive stuff?"

"Yes, explosive stuff. Massively explosive. ZIFs themselves are merely a matrix of nanoparticles. However, ZIFs have an advantage over other and similar materials in that they can be produced easily, quickly, and at room temperature. In and of themselves, they're not necessarily dangerous. However, the relative ease with which they can be concocted, combined with, shall we say, an interesting affinity for combination with other agents to produce a hypergolic material—"

"Hypergolic?"

"A fuel, say, or an explosive that spontaneously ignites. It usually refers to two materials, such as hydrazine, which is the stuff they use in air bags, and some type of nitrogen compound. Put the two together in enough quantity and circumstance and you have the space shuttle.

The advantage ZIFs provides is that unlike hydrazine, for example, which is toxic stuff and causes all kinds of birth defects, ZIFs are not as poisonous. Not that this is the prime attractor. ZIFs can achieve great kinetics in much smaller packages due to their nanometal structure."

"Meaning," Jim said, "a big bomb in a small package."

"Or an unlimited fuel tank for a space craft, but, yes, a compact bomb, too."

"You said he was smart, I guess."

"Yes, he's very smart. But he's also more than a little off, you know? Everything he thinks about seems to have to do with blowing things up. It's scary."

"He's an SLK . . ."

"Exactly, Officer. My professional opinion exactly."

They laughed together again.

After another coffee, Malinda asked if Jim was up for something to eat.

"Hummus and pita chips are about the only edible thing on the menu," she said. "But they're pretty good."

Jim didn't mind that coffee was turning into dinner, even if it was chips and dip.

"Let me ask you one more thing," he said after they'd ordered. "Kevin White. Football player. Wrestler. What do you know about him?"

Malinda shook her head. "Those knuckleheads. They're all protected by the coaches. White is a particular pain in my ass."

"Why?" Jim asked.

"Midterm grades come out next week. Most teachers give the top athletes a pass. You know, C-minus and done. Me, too, usually. But this time, I just can't do it. He goes too far."

"A D?" Jim asked.

"Worse. Try a big fat F. Foxtrot to you, soldier boy."

"So, what happens then?"

"First, I get his mother. She'll be up my

chimney in a South Side second. Then the wrestling coach, a little balding guy who gives me the total creeps."

"Why the coach?"

"Can't participate in a sport if you're failing a main-halls course."

"Main halls?"

"English, science, social studies, math."

"I see."

"He won't be able to keep wrestling, the big palooka, and I'll get blamed for that, I assure you."

The waitress set down a large bowl of a creamy tan dip, surrounded by an array of soft pita triangles. Jim had never tried hummus before and timidly dipped one of the wedges into the chickpea puree.

"Not bad," he said, enthusiastically reaching for another.

Malinda scooted her chair closer. "I have to tell you something," she whispered, and his hand paused at the dip bowl. Then before he knew it, Malinda's lips were on his, warm and soft. Her tongue slipped across his upper lip, and when she pulled away, she said, "You had a little splotch of hummus."

Jim's fingers shot up to his lip, but there was nothing left to wipe away. It had been some time since he had been kissed, and his body buzzed with nerves and excitement. He relaxed a little as Malinda grabbed a slice of pita and took a bite herself. They ate mostly in silence, regarding each other thoughtfully.

The waitress cleared away the dip bowl and Malinda ordered them each an IPA. Jim wished he'd known the place served beer from the be-ginning. That would have made things easier.

A different waitress from before set down their pints, then knelt and lit the table candle in the red, bulb-shaped glass. When she'd gone, Malinda slid her chair even closer and leaned toward him. Their lips met again and a flood of happiness coursed through Jim. They remained at the corner table in the shadows, drinking beer and kissing. Nobody in the place seemed to mind that they were making out. Jim decided he liked the Blackbird Café. Rather a lot.

The next morning Jim walked down the south hallway. Malinda's door was shut. He caught a glimpse of her dark hair through the rectangular window in the door. She was at her desk, grading lab reports. He knocked.

"I was thinking maybe we could get some more hummus tonight," Jim said.

"I don't want you to think I'm slutty."

"Slutty isn't a term that comes to mind."

They went back and forth over a place to meet. With each suggestion, Jim felt increasingly provincial compared to Malinda's sophistication. It sounded as if she'd been to every trendy upstate bar Jim had ever read about in the *NorWIN* weekly free alternative paper.

"How about the Derringer?" she asked finally. The Derringer was a trendy brew pub in an old roadhouse in Wheeler, which was little more than a railroad grade on the Chicago, Fort Wayne, and Eastern.

"Wear your uniform," Malinda said.

"I can't drink in my uniform," Jim said.

"What a pity," she said. "What else can you do out of uniform?"

3

Patti Triplett was drumming her manicured nails on her desk when Jim entered the administration office. Jim couldn't disagree with Tom Harbaugh's proclamation that Patti was hot, and he didn't mind Tom's tendency to call her Hot Patti when she was out of earshot. She was hot. But he found Tom's reasoning too simplistic. There was something more to her than just long legs, tight skirts, and a deeply suspicious tan.

"Hey, there, Officer Jim," she said.

"Patti, come on," Jim said. "You make me feel like a jerk with the 'Officer' stuff."

"Okay," she said with a mischievous grin. "Jim-boy."

"Whatever," he chuckled. "Can I have the disciplinary records for two students? Nygard, Karsten, and White, Kevin?"

"You may," she said as she pushed back from her desk. "Two of our finest juniors."

The student records were kept, according to the dictates of FERPA, in a locked storage room. Patti had a key that hung from a red lanyard around her neck.

She returned from the file room with two red folders, reading one as she pulled the door shut behind her.

"Quite the fellow," she said. It wasn't clear which student she referred to. She slapped both folders down on the counter. "You'll be needing to come behind the Great Wall of China here to look at them," she said. "Rules are rules."

"I'm allowed back there?"

"You are now," she said and smiled.

There were all sorts of rumors about Hot Patti around the school. She dated a cop. She was married to an older man who owned a NASCAR team. According to graffiti in the girls' toilets, she was a lesbian. The graffiti in the boys' toilets took an opposite and more obscene slant.

Jim picked the two folders off the counter. Patti gestured toward a small gray desk pushed against a wall at the far end of the office. It was known colloquially as the One Call Desk, where students were sent to call their parents before the inevitable storm of discipline and detention came down on them.

Jim began with Kevin White.

Despite the gold chain and sleeveless gray sweatshirts, Kevin came from a privileged background. He had even attended the fancy private elementary and middle schools in Schererville before he enrolled at Portage.

His grades were predictably mediocre. The

academic reports were thin and mostly pro forma. He was an unexceptional student prone to being unfocused and disruptive in a minor way. He scraped along in all his subjects equally. There were no shining exceptions. He had yet to make an appointment for college counseling.

Sports were another story. He had played JV football as a freshman and made varsity as a sophomore. In training camp the following summer, he broke an arm in practice. This was all the file noted of the incident. After his sophomore football season, he had filled out the preliminary forms indicating an interest in recruitment for collegiate sports. While there had been no further update on that front, this past season he'd been a stand-out player as Portage made it to the 6A semi-finals. He'd started as an offensive tackle and saw time on special teams and as a second-string linebacker.

His wrestling career was equally impressive. As a freshman he'd hit the mat at 172 pounds, but he'd bulked up and was now a heavyweight. His junior season was off to a solid start, with four wins under his belt, including two pins.

Malinda was right; if he failed chemistry and got kicked off the team, the coach would be pissed.

In terms of disciplinary actions, there was a stack of pink parking ticket counterfoils. All of them, it appeared, had been paid with checks from his mother, often in clumps of eight to ten tickets. On a later page, a notation was made of his having damaged school property, specifically a student locker in the science hallway. It didn't say whose or how it had been damaged. There were also three mentions of being part of larger groups of boys detained and then ejected from basketball games with local rivals. In his freshman year a freshman girl had complained of unwanted and harassing attention.

Jim's eyebrows rose when he saw the name of the girl who'd filed the complaint: Amber

Parker. He was surprised yet not surprised at the same time.

He closed and set aside Kevin White's red folder then opened the one on Karsten Nygard.

Karsten's father was an associate professor of engineering at Purdue University. His mother, also an engineer, had recently started a new position in a lab at Notre Dame. Before that she had listed her work address as the GMC Labs in Michigan City.

Karsten's grades were perfect, excepting those in physical education. A medical letter sent in the fall of his freshman year indicated that, due to physical limitations resulting from a childhood illness, he should be exempted from courses of an athletic nature.

The notes from teachers were far more copious than those found in Kevin White's folder. Mostly they expounded on the superior quality of Karsten's work, and for many his single-minded pursuit of perfection was the only worrying concern. Other teachers took a dimmer view of Karsten's laser focus on academics.

"Spectrum?" one teacher scribbled.

"IEP appropriate?" noted another in his freshman year, referring to the independent educational plans created for students with disabilities.

"Personality/psychological disorder?" wrote another.

"Difficult home situation, I gather," wrote a fourth.

He had been disciplined on occasion, usually after lashing out at other students for teasing or making fun. He aroused protectiveness in the teachers who worried about him. Others found him quirky and annoying. He spoke little and kept to himself. He was a question mark, a concern, and a bit of a mystery.

In other words, he was a suspect.

***

Jim left the office and strode through the west lobby and down the north hallway to Chuck Marlow's classroom. It was now third period and Marlow sat at the head of his empty seating scheme, scribbling in a broad hand with a fountain pen over student papers he pulled from one pile and then tossed onto another.

"There was another bombing," Jim said.

"I think, with your experience, you'd agree that *bombing* is a bit hysterical a term for high school pranking."

"Well, I guess," Jim said. "But a junior girl did get hurt recently, or at least pretty shook up. And yesterday an explosion went off close enough to this kid Kevin White that, a few steps closer, it could have been real trouble."

"Kevin White," Marlow said. "Now there's trouble. At the least he's an incipient case of borderline personality disorder. If he isn't a full-blown sociopath already."

"Maybe. But he's a victim, too. He got back-fire exhaust all down the side of his precious white Ford. I don't think even a budding socio-path would streak his own pickup."

"The kid is trouble," Marlow repeated. "Never underestimate a man with a personality disorder."

"One of the chemistry teachers flagged Karsten Nygard to me. You know the drill: She finds him to be 'kind of quiet. Keeps to him-self.' He also demonstrates a keen interest in explosives."

"A troubled soul," Marlow said. "Nothing more, nothing less. The kid is harmless."

"So, you're not concerned?" Jim asked.

"With Karsten Nygard or Kevin White?"

"Nygard," Jim said.

"No, not Nygard. That sort doesn't kill. He

doesn't blow people up. The only person that type ever hurts is himself. And only after being hounded by the Kevin Whites of the world."

"Is there some history between the two?"

"The White kid, so I hear," Marlow said, "put hands on Karsten the other day."

"At Skateland?" Jim asked, piecing together the bits of a rumor he'd heard.

"I really don't know the names of the local fleshpots, Jim."

"Because I heard a kid got beat up at the skate rink."

"Somebody is always getting beaten up at the skate rink. This is Indiana. A state of barren parking lots and blood-flecked truck bumpers."

"Okay, fair enough."

Marlow waved a hand. "This, too, will pass. Nygard is not your man."

"I don't know. He just seems—"

"Don't worry," Marlow said. "See you at lunch next week."

"See you at lunch," Jim repeated. "Sure."

As Jim left Marlow's classroom, Amber entered. "Hi, Jim," she said brightly as she passed. "Mr. Marlow! We still on for our Mr. Marlow Lunch today?"

Marlow's reply was lost as Jim returned to his office, taking the south hallway so he could sneak a glance through Malinda's rectangular window. She stood at the lab benches holding an Erlenmeyer flask filled with smoking red goo.

He continued past the lines of lockers, pausing for a moment to take in the scene in the west lobby. Students milled around the entrance to the cafeteria, the ones entering pawing their pockets for their meal vouchers. Those leaving, mainly the boys, crushed their pint milk cartons and tossed them with varying degrees of accuracy into the big rubber trash cans just inside the doors.

He strode toward the SRO office, passing the admin suite, where he could see Hot Patti through the plate-glass windows, her head down as she filled out paperwork. The lights above glinted off her blond hair.

He pulled open the SRO office door and found Tom Harbaugh thumbing through a copy of *Great Lakes Magazine*. "What's up?" Tom asked distractedly.

"I read their files, White and Nygard," Jim said.

"It's not White," Tom replied quickly. "I may just be fish and game, but that much I know. Nobody bombs his own truck."

"I don't know," Jim said. "Not a lot makes sense with that kid."

"And Karsten Nygard is some kind of open book?"

"He's worse," Jim agreed. "Maybe it's neither of them."

"Oh, great," Tom said. "That's just ducky."

Hot Patti stuck her head into the small room. Tom immediately became flustered. He sat up too quickly, nearly knocking his cup of Circle K coffee off the desk. He smushed shut his magazine like he'd been caught with a porno by his mom.

"There's been a murder in the cafeteria," Patti announced in a theatrical voice. Tom's crazed expression grew. "That food they serve. Did you see today's version of sloppy joes? Homicidal!"

It occurred to Jim as he drove to the Derringer why Malinda had chosen to meet in Wheeler. It was almost exactly halfway between their places, so neither would have to drive farther than the other after their drink. And neither of their places would be particularly inconvenient to go to for a nightcap.

But it was early, he told himself. Early days.

They found a small table in the bar area.

"Grain Belt, please," Malinda said to the waitress.

"Grain Belt?" Jim couldn't hide his astonishment. "Are you serious?"

"What are you, a beer snob?"

"No, I'm not, it just seems like an, I don't know, eccentric choice. Do they even have Grain Belt here? Isn't it out of Wisconsin or something?"

"We have it," the waitress said.

"It's from Minnesota," Malinda clarified. Both women looked at him impatiently.

"Okay, okay." Jim held up both hands in surrender. "I'll have one, too."

The waitress brought them two bottles of Grain Belt Elite and two glasses.

"Aren't you glad I ordered this?" Malinda gave him a teasing smile as she poured the light-yellow lager. "Cheers!"

They clinked and Jim took a tentative sip.

He wasn't sure if it was the color or flavor, but he instantly thought of corn. Not what he was expecting, but tasty. Kind of like Malinda.

His gaze met hers over their glasses and his stomach went wobbly as he caught a flirtatious glint in her eye. He set down his drink on a coaster, expecting her to do the same, but was surprised to see she was steadily gulping down the beer in one fell swoop. A small burp erupted from her lips when she was done, and she laughed.

"Oops. Sorry. Not very ladylike." She wiped a streak of foam off her lip with a paper napkin and stared at him. "You ready?"

Jim was baffled. They had just gotten there. But he looked down at his mostly full beer and shrugged. "I mean, I guess. Sure."

As they ventured into the dark and cold evening, a clanking diesel car carrier lumbered across the grade on the other side of Highway 130. Malinda had parked right next to Jim.

"Follow me," Malinda said.

"Follow you where?"

"Where do you think, big boy?"

Jim could almost hear his heart thudding over the sound of the whizzing traffic. "Just don't speed. I don't want to have to arrest you," he said in an awkward attempt at humor and immediately regretted it.

Malinda lived in an old building in downtown Valparaiso called the Calyx Hotel. It sat across the street from the public library and two blocks off the courthouse square.

"It was never a hotel," she clarified as she unlocked the door to the checkered-floor lobby.

Her apartment had wooden floors, oriental rugs, furniture she'd probably bought herself from an actual furniture store, and real paintings on the walls. It was clean and classy. Starkly different from anywhere Jim had ever lived. The scents of teak and oolong tea hung in the air.

She snapped on a lamp made from a Chinese pot sitting on a table covered with books. After slipping out of her down jacket she reached to take Jim's coat. Her black slacks and turtleneck sweater hugged her figure, and her dark hair glowed in the soft light. She sank onto an upholstered loveseat and propped her brown boots on a low coffee table.

"Now, Officer," she said. "You can arrest me."

The Mr. Marlow Lunch, as it was called by the students, was legendary. Once each trimester, all his students were taken out, in safe groups of two or three, by Mr. Marlow to lunch. He paid, and the restaurants he chose were nice. The Parade, Cuda's, The Rosebud. It wasn't fine dining, exactly, but it was a few steps above what high school students were accustomed to. And, in some cases, it was the nicest meal out they had ever enjoyed.

Today was Jim's turn for a Mr. Marlow Lunch of sorts, though neither man called it by the nickname.

Jim found Chuck in his classroom, sitting, as always, behind an enormous and unruly stack of student papers.

"Jim Lord," he said, rising to his feet. He snatched a jacket from the back of his oak swivel banker's chair. Most certainly not standard issue, like the mission-style table that would serve as his desk if it weren't buried under newspapers and magazines.

"Flight jacket," Jim noted.

"I told you I fly."

Jim followed Marlow out of the building, across the Skirt, and to the faculty lot. Marlow stopped beside an old blue Volvo then drove them south through Wheeler and then southwest to the red brick gates of a country club.

"It used to be called the Gary Works Supervisor's Club," he explained as he steered along the drive toward the clubhouse. The course was closed and the trees bare, but the lines of the fairways were clear. They came to a stop outside a Georgian-style brick building, ornately quoined at every corner. "It gives you an idea of how well even supervisors did at the height of US Steel."

"I wonder what the Manager's Club looks like?" Jim quipped. He was rewarded with a chuckle.

"You need to go up to Chicago for those," Marlow said. "Medinah. Kemper Lakes. Places where Majors are held. Tiger won the PGA twice at Medinah."

"So, you golf?"

"What kind of question is that? Of course, I golf. What, you don't?"

"I guess I never learned. Never had the chance, really."

"It is a state of mind, golf is. But also all the

exclusionary, upper-crust stuff that gets said about it."

After the valet took the car and they went inside, the woman standing at the podium in front of the mostly empty dining room called Marlow by name and gave him a warm hug.

"This place doesn't seem like you," Jim remarked once they were seated, water glasses filled, and a basket of warm bread deposited.

"The course is better than I am," Marlow said. "For me, that's enough."

"And all the other perks?"

"Oh, I'm just here for the golf. I eat here a couple of times a month to cover the minimums. Sometimes on a hot summer afternoon I'll bring a book and sit for a while beside the pool. A lot of the girls from Culver Academy hang out here summers."

Jim raised his eyebrows.

"What? I was once young and full of life," Marlow said. "I'll bring you out when the course opens for the season. You're a good shot, I suppose?"

"Sharpshooter badge. In basic training."

"There's a lot that's the same. The steady hands. The centering. I think you'd take to it well. There's a lot to be said for a long walk across a pretty lawn." Then he said as though there could be no argument, "You're going to come out with me flying. We don't need to wait for the weather to warm up for that."

"You've got a plane?"

Marlow shrugged. "Well, that's a long story. Most of the time, I use one that belongs to the club. They have four or maybe five. One is usually available. I like their new Piper Archer. It's fun."

"Where do you go?"

"Here and there, back and forth. I have a route I like, up the lake. On good days, it can be so clear you can see the bottom. Really! Up past the skyline and then to Milwaukee.

There's a nice municipal strip up there. Close by there's a Greek steak house that serves stuffed cabbage rolls and boiled ribs and sauerkraut. Heaven. Milwaukee German food in a Greek steak house at an airport. Can you think of anything better?"

"Sauerkraut? Cabbage rolls?"

"Come on." Marlow laughed as the waitress served steaming bowls of lobster bisque, a club specialty. "A Gary boy like you must have eaten his fair share of bratwurst and sauerkraut."

"My grandmother at Thanksgiving. Sauerkraut stewed with giblets. Never went near it."

"That's a delicacy, you dummy!"

"I guess. Then what. Fly back?"

"Sure. I come back down what's called the Bojack Route. West of Chicago. With the afternoon sun picking out the buildings, their shadows running for miles out over the lake. It's a wonder."

"I've never been in a small plane like that," Jim mused.

"You'll love it," Marlow promised.

"I was wondering more about what you did in the Navy."

"Navy stuff. *Gungy*," he said with a growl.

"How long were you in?"

Marlow took a few enthusiastic spoonfuls of bisque, then dabbed his lip with a cloth napkin from his lap. He shrugged again. "A big chunk of it I worked for the State Department. Some of that time I was in, maybe? Then I went into the reserves."

"Okay." Jim wondered how far to press. "What did you do at State?"

"Training," Marlow said, returning to his bowl of coral pink soup. "I traveled a lot."

Navy Special Ops, State Department, and lots of travel. Jim began to get the picture.

The waitress cleared the soup course, then brought out two Supervisor's Burgers. Marlow had told him they were made purely from prime tenderloin scraps, and by the look of Jim's, he certainly agreed it fell in the upper register of burgers.

"Where did the State stuff take place?"

"When I started, it was Belgium. Those were great times—all of Europe just steps away. I'd work the week in Brussels and then spend the weekend trout fishing in Scotland."

Jim tried to figure the probable dates in his head as he took a bite from the massive burger, ordered rare at Marlow's insistence. It was tender and juicy, a clear step above his usual fast-food fare.

"After that, they moved me to Central America. That was where I had to work, I mean, really work. Those were some busy days."

Somehow Jim knew this was the natural limit of what he was going to learn about Chuck Marlow's professional career.

"And afterward?"

"When you start early, you hit your number early. I came back up here to see after my mother who was getting on. Family stuff. The teaching was a lark, a favor for a friend, supposedly a short tour. But here I am."

Jim had a small sheet with Karsten Nygard's course schedule on it. It was a hieroglyph: Calc BC, Physics C: Mechanics, Computer Science A, Microeconomics. Unlike most students, who took their break around the middle of the day, Karsten had slotted his in his second period.

The computer science lab was a stale and windowless room in the center of the building where the south and B hallways met. Two rows of white-topped tables ran down the middle of the room, each with a workstation on it. Recessed fluorescent lights burned above and the walls were lined in whiteboards covered in palimpsests of programming scribbles never fully erased. Snack bags, evidence of forbidden food, littered the carpet. The air had the terrible smell of flop sweat.

A scrawny kid was hunched over a keyboard.

"Karsten?" Jim asked, poking his head in from the hall.

The teen looked up from his computer. On the screen before him ran lines and lines of type in blues and oranges. "What?" he asked.

"I'm Officer Lord. I don't think we've met yet. What are you working on?"

"CS homework."

Jim pulled out a rolling seat a table away and sat. "I hear you're president of the Model Rocket Club."

"I'm the sole member of the Model Rocket Club," Karsten corrected. "We didn't have an election."

Jim had a moment of sympathy. There was something about the stereotype, the archetype, maybe, that never appeared to change. Karsten played the dork. His dark hair was combed over and greasy. His glasses looked flimsy; the rectangular lenses were cheap photosensitive plastic, frozen perpetually at a pale shade of gray. Jim could see pale wisps of black down on his jaw and chin, made more definite by his otherwise ghostly white skin. An overstuffed canvas backpack sat at his feet, an open paper lunch sack sneaking out of the zipper opening.

"I did some of that when I was a kid," Jim said. He immediately felt lame. "Estes kits, rockets, that stuff."

"Model Rocket Club is a misleading title," Karsten said. "Obviously it's all robotics and drones now."

"Oh," Jim said. "Right."

A long silence hung between them. Karsten sat utterly without affect, his hands pressed between the thighs of his outlet blue jeans.

"It's all totally legal," Karsten said finally. "If that's what you're after."

Defeated, Jim stood and pushed the roller chair back into the workstation.

"No doubt," he said. "I have no doubt it is."

He had mixed feelings about the defiant kid seated in front of him. Karsten was clearly someone who pushed people away, even—or maybe especially—sympathetic ones. At the same time, he hardly came off as a person who would hurt others with anything other than his sarcastic wit.

Jim and Malinda met for an early supper at a place called Sportsman's, named because it had once, when Jim was a kid, been a sporting goods store. There had been sections, like little countries, he remembered thinking, dedicated by sport: baseball and football, tennis and golf, fishing and hunting. For a long time, the building sat empty, victim of box stores and an eccentric owner who probably had been conked on the helmet one too many times playing left guard down at State. The new owners did the minimum of rehab. The same yellowed linoleum tiles covered the floor, and the outside went untouched, down to the splashy neon sign that spelled SPORTSMAN'S vertically. The jumping trout below had long since stopped jumping.

Jim and Malinda liked it because it had a rough reputation. It wasn't that they preferred the bikers and chronically unemployed construction types it catered to, but because Portage High kids rarely went there. They could eat and talk without risk of being bothered.

"I'm even more worried about Karsten," Malinda said. "He just seems worse every day. Withdrawn. Morose."

"I ran into him today. We talked a little."

"You got a word out of him?

Their food came in checkered deli paper–lined red plastic baskets. Jim had ordered the fish fry. Malinda had gone for the special, a massive hamburger. This version was not about quality of beef, like at the Supervisor's Club. This was about a half-pound of fatty ground chuck, balled, fried, and slathered in comeback sauce.

Jim chased a bite of fish with a few fries before continuing his train of thought. "What if he's got some grudge and turns out to be the next Dylan Klebold?"

"The Columbine kid?"

"There is such a thing as Columbine copycats. Kids who study it obsessively and plan their own attack accordingly."

"I thought that was Japanese kids," she said.

"You're thinking of Korean kids who sleep in caskets as a way of not killing themselves."

"By the way, there's a Korean barbecue place over in Hammond we should try. You know, the kind of place where there's a charcoal pit set in the middle of your table and they bring you pork belly and thin strips of beef and stuff like that, and you cook it yourself and then eat it wrapped up in a leaf of lettuce."

Jim had this jealous thought that Malinda had a line of sophisticated old boyfriends behind her, brainy Midwestern sorts, whom she'd been dating since moving to Valparaiso. The sort of guys she went with to places like Korean barbecue restaurants in Hammond and talked to about books.

"I told you I went through Karsten's record," he said. "Okay, he's a nerd. A dork. He looks funny and dresses funny. His mother and his father aren't around much, working down at Purdue and over at Notre Dame. He's a little off, sure, but he also seems gentle. I mean, because he's smart, suddenly he's a bomber?"

"With an interest in ZIFs?" Malinda asked. "Uh, yes. He's a bomber. No normal seventeen-year-old has an interest in that stuff. Think about it. This is sophisticated hypergolics. MIT stuff. NASA stuff. We're not talking about Team Whatever or gophers and goblins. You know, normal teenage stuff. We're talking about an active and practical interest in detonative materials characterized by their light weight, ease of handling, and *detonative capacities*, Jim. Like, *boom!*" Her fingers danced in the air beside her face like fireworks.

"He's just mixed up," Jim said.

"Hot Patti tell you that?"

Jim hadn't known the nickname extended beyond the SRO office. He shook his head and felt himself blushing. "No, Patti Triplett didn't tell me anything. I mean, she showed me the . . . oh, never mind." He crammed a few more fries into his mouth. "My point is, there's nothing obvious in his record. Just a bunch of little pieces. There's no single thread. There's no line stringing them together. Maybe there really are no grounds for a referral."

"Oh, Jim, you dummy." Malinda smiled

ruefully. "Go ahead. Have it your way. And if Karsten comes to school one day with a backpack full of zinc and some white fuming nitric acid—that's a *bomb* to you, Jim—and he blows up the place? If, with the flick of one little switch, he turns all of Portage High School into something looking like Launch Pad 39A? Without the suppression system? What do we do then? Say we had no idea? That we never saw it coming?"

"Karsten is being picked on," Jim said. "He's being bullied by people like Kevin White."

Malinda took a huge bite of her burger, as big and round as a softball. Jim marveled at the way she could eat, as if tomorrow would never come. Since getting back from Iraq, Jim had begun watching his weight. Malinda, who was slim and fit, ate like a Hoosier.

"Somdy . . ." she started unsuccessfully, then took a moment to finish chewing. She grabbed a paper napkin and wiped sauce off her chin.

"Somebody has got to do something about Karsten. Being bullied, Officer, is one of the reasons high school students *blow things up!*"

"I don't know what more I can do," Jim said. "Short of finding an actual bomb in his backpack."

"Whatever. The kid practically has 'suicide bomber' written on his forehead."

"I feel for him. Having the Malinda Murches of the world against him."

"I'm not *against* him." She frowned. "He's just not a *cool* kid."

"*Crash and splash,*" Jim muttered to himself, then said more loudly, "What am I going to do? This is just my luck. First SRO duty, now a mass murderer? And some poor, dorky kid getting blamed for it all?"

"Your luck was to meet me." Malinda narrowed her eyes and raised her eyebrows. "Have you got a problem with that?"

"None at all."

"*Then make sure I don't get blown up!*" She clutched his forearm, giving it a squeeze. "You don't want to lose me, do you?"

"I don't," he said, covering her hand with his. He suddenly felt like he might cry. He looked down at the greasy piece of fish remaining in his basket and blinked a few times. "I really don't want to lose you."

A little nervous for reasons he couldn't identify, Jim drove to the Gary airport, Gary International, as it was facetiously if factually called. It was a cloudless Saturday, and an Arctic high sat with its center directly over Northern Indiana. Marlow waited in his running car, scribbling on an FAA chart.

"Good," he said, climbing from the blue Volvo. "I just filed our flight plan."

Jim followed Marlow through an empty terminal to a desk at the back. A young man talking on his phone waved to Marlow and pointed to a manila folder on the counter before him. Marlow gave him a thumbs-up and pushed through a nearby door.

"Severe clear," Marlow said, "as my first flight instructor liked to say. CAVU: ceiling and visibility unlimited."

Jim followed as Marlow did his preflight check. The young man who had been on the phone came running out across the apron. He and Marlow engaged in some shop talk, inscrutable to Jim. Then, far more quickly than he thought possible, the propeller spooled up and they were bumping across the tarmac to the taxiway. Through the headphones, he listened as Marlow communicated with the tower, speaking in that clipped and military way that was so opposite the near-Midwestern drawl Marlow used when conversing casually.

The plane felt alive beneath them. It jiggled

and bounced. Marlow moved the flaps and wiggled the ailerons and flapped the rudder.

"Cleared for takeoff, nine-eight-nine-November."

"Nine-eight-nine-November, cleared for take-off."

Within a fraction of the time it took on a commercial flight, Jim began to see the ground fall away beneath him. The target stripes flashed. Below lay the tidy grid of the white tanks of the Citgo fuel farm, then the closely built lozenge of East Chicago. Marlow banked right and leveled as they flew directly over a riverboat casino. Then came the brown sprawl of the old Gary Works, followed by the nearly moribund but still smoking here and there towers of the US Steel plant. Then a hard line and the beginning of the beach and tawny sands of the Indiana seashore, where Jim had played most summers as a child. Marlow charted a course low and parallel with the shore. Jim kept his nose pressed to the window.

Marlow flew the Piper along the coast as far as Muskegon before making a wide, curving turn out over the lake and vectoring them back to Gary. As the shoreline came into clearer view and Marlow prepared for landing, Jim's spirit soared with the plane, enlivened and animated by all the possibility that sprawled to the horizon. *CAVU, indeed,* he thought.

"This takes things off your mind, doesn't it?"

"It does," Jim said. "It really does."

"As I said, it's good to get out from time to time."

Jim was alone in the cramped SRO office a couple of weeks later, filling out paperwork, when Hot Patti again stuck her blond head inside the door.

"Patti," Jim said. "What's up?"

"We could have made sweet music together, Officer Jim." She twirled a bright red fingertip around a strand of hair. "It's a dang shame."

"Get out, Patti," Jim said, chuckling but flattered. He had to admit she looked good, even if standing naked inside a light bulb and getting your skin fried struck him as a bad idea. "You know that never would have happened."

"Try me sometime," she said. "You know where I hide."

He couldn't quite figure what she was spoofing about. Hot Patti was a firecracker, but this was fresh even for her. Jim realized he had never gotten the real story on her. "I thought you had a boyfriend, Patti. A cop."

"A cop?" She snorted but took it as an invitation to step inside and perch on the edge of Jim's desk. "My *brother* is a *state trooper*," she said. "Which is why I'd never date a cop in, like, a billion years."

"Well, I'm a cop," Jim said. "So."

"Ha! You are a kinder-cop, James. A hall monitor with a badge."

"That kind of hurts, Patti." It did a little.

"I would go out with you, though," she said. "I mean it. If it weren't for that *slattern* in the science hallway."

"You mean Mr. Mark?" Lance Mark was a bearded mystery who taught Chemistry I and II. Each weekend he commuted all the way downstate to work on his family's farm where they had been growing soybean but were considering hemp.

"You know exactly to whom I refer."

"'Slattern'? That's a bit harsh, isn't it?"

"Tart, chippy, moll, what have you?"

"Okay. Let's do it. When are we getting together?"

"Us?" she said, pointing between them. "Me and you?"

"Sure, me, us, like you just said. Go out. Do something together."

"No way, José. I don't want Mindy Murch crawling down my hidey hole. She scares me. I don't want to die."

Jim smiled.

"But that's the only reason," she said. "The *only* reason." She winked, and Jim knew it was time to change the subject.

"Tell me what you really think about Karsten Nygard."

Hot Patti's lips curled down from coy to contemplative and her brow furrowed briefly. "I think he's a sweet doofus with no friends who wears flood pants and gets picked on by the dumb jocks of the world."

Jim might not have phrased it quite like that, but he felt the same way. "You're actually a kind person under all that mid-winter tan, aren't you?"

"You should have come to me first, Jim. We

could have made beautiful music together." Patti spun on her heel, almost knocking her head on the doorframe, and sashayed out the door.

Jim smiled again as she gently closed it behind her.

4

Jim pulled into one of the two parking spots reserved for SROs in the administration and faculty lot. It was a beautiful morning. A warm front had cleared the mid-February drear, and the sun sparkled at the edge of a bright blue sky.

Tom Harbaugh pulled in right after him.

"Hey, Jim, my man. Favor time?" Tom was in a good mood as they got out of their vehicles. "Would you mind if I cut out right at loading? You cover? The wife wants me to go shopping for baby stuff."

More than a month had passed with no further explosions—pranks, Jim had come to agree with Marlow—since the episode with Kevin White's truck, and it was a half day at Portage: the end of the second trimester. Students would be released early, and teachers had the afternoon to mark and submit their final grading for the term.

Jim had hoped to get away early himself, but Malinda told him she had a "short ton" of grading left, not to mention chewing over what to do about Kevin White's poor performance. Jim might hang around and wait for her. Their relationship was at the point where he didn't much think of doing things without her.

Despite his initial reservations, Jim had come to appreciate Tom Harbaugh and his down-home, Department of Natural Services–officer simplicity. Jim now took to gladly hearing about his wife's daily progress in her pregnancy. He found Tom's goofy exuberance and surprisingly detailed anxieties endearing.

"Sure," he said. "Knock yourself out. Where are you going?"

"There's a Baby Barn up in Michigan City. Jim, do you know how much this stuff *costs*?"

"I don't." Jim chuckled, recalling the last thing Tom had complained about the price of: dildos. Quite the mash-up with cribs and car seats. "I've never considered it."

"Well, it's a lot, believe me." Tom absently smoothed the crease in his khaki trousers, worn with a new SRO polo Jim hadn't seen before. Jim was dressed in his blues. "And the weather today! On a half day!"

It was unseasonably warm and forecast to be so for the entire day. False spring.

"You tell the office yet?" Jim asked.

"I left Hot Patti a message last night. She hasn't called, so I guess it's no biggie."

The early-arrival students were rambunctious. The combination of the half day, the end of the trimester, and the promising weather contributed to giving everyone a touch of giddiness.

The morning went by without lunch bells. At 12:30, last bells rang for the day. The students were loud and happy.

Jim made extra hall patrols. Hijinks of one sort or another were likely with spirits so ebullient.

Chuck Marlow was standing outside his classroom, holding the door partially open. His worshipful students filed out, wishing him a good weekend. Amber Parker was last and paused beside him. She said something Jim couldn't hear, but it garnered a smile from her teacher as she continued down the hall.

Jim didn't hate his job so much at times like those. The students seemed happy, carefree even. They were good kids looking forward to a few days off from school.

In the distance, at the end of the A hallway,

Jim caught a glimpse of Tom, headed out early. Tom waved exaggeratedly, a hokey smile lighting up his face.

At the junction with the B hall, Jim passed Karsten Nygard in a floppy Doctor Who hat and a black raincoat. His skinny frame couldn't weigh more than a hundred pounds wet.

Jim felt for the kid. He was never going to be anything in high school but a weirdo and an outcast. Maybe for his entire life. Jim sensed a lot of himself in Karsten. He had never belonged, either. He was the orphan. The kid who grew up with his grandparents. The cop who was of so little account he got put on SRO duty at a high school. Karsten came out of a different mold, but he was the same flavor.

After school Jim covered the bus lanes as the students boarded without incident, eager to get home. He considered dropping by Malinda's classroom to say hello, but he knew that if he left her alone she'd finalize her grades quicker. So instead, he busied himself with paperwork while waiting patiently for her to text him so they could leave together, for whatever adventure she had dreamed up to mark the end of the term.

While he was rereading his notes in the daily log, a sharp report rang out, shaking the lockers on their hinges in the hallway outside his open door. He jumped to his feet and sprinted to the east lobby, where the familiar odor of burnt hobby rocket fuel assaulted his nostrils. The lobby was deserted and the windows were all intact, but in a corner he spotted the same black scorch marks he'd seen beneath Kevin White's pickup truck.

Jim stared at the floor, trying to make sense of it. The car bomb prankster had brought his act indoors. Why here, in the east lobby, and why now? With the school mostly empty? The only people left were some athletes, cheer-leaders, and a few club-goers. Maybe part of the pep band.

At that moment a series of short blasts reverberated through the lobby. Jim wheeled around and raced toward the sound of semi-automatic gunshots as a grim realization struck him: The explosion in the east lobby had been a diversionary tactic. It was intended to get him, or Tom Harbaugh, or whoever, away from the west lobby and the cafeteria. The place in the school where on a day like that day most of the remaining students would be.

As Jim got closer, the shots slowed, as if the shooter was becoming more deliberate, select-ing targets and aiming between shots. The sound still echoed off the lockers, and there were so many hallways, he couldn't tell where it was coming from.

Jim held at the corner of the south hall-way and took a breath to steady himself. He swept his thumb over the safety on his gun and rounded the corner with it drawn. For the first time since his SRO duty had begun, he felt like a real cop.

He peeked around the corner and found the west lobby empty. He exhaled audibly, but as he glanced through the open door to the admin suite, his breath caught. Sheets of printer paper were fanned out on the carpet, splattered with red. The swinging partition was blocked open, and a trickle of crimson streamed past a pink high heel. Beyond it, blood pooled under Hot Patti's crumpled form, her blond hair still flawlessly styled as her eyes stared lifelessly at the ceiling.

Big saucer eyes, suddenly staring out from a soldier's body, limp and blood-spattered and wrapped in yellow insulation as Jim carried the litter to the medic tent.

Thock-thock-thock.

Jim blinked in alarm but saw only the office

and Patti when his focus returned. Then another shot rang out and he darted inside, squatting behind the door to stay hidden so he could think. There had been an explosion in the north corner of the east lobby, then a shooting in the south corner of the west lobby. Shots were still being fired, but where was the perpetrator?

Jim steeled himself and stepped out from his cover, service weapon at the ready. Footsteps echoed from the far end of the west lobby, and from the north hall emerged a lone figure, dressed for the part in a black T-shirt, black jeans, and black boots under a black trench coat. A sturdy black backpack was strapped to the teen's back and he wore yellow-tinted shooting glasses and noise-canceling headphones as he strode purposefully toward the cafeteria. He gripped an AK-17 with authority, and between his teeth he clenched a black string that appeared to be coming from his shoulder.

Why is he chewing on a string? Jim wondered for the briefest moment, before realization set in. It wasn't a string. It was a ripcord. A ripcord that led to the backpack, which probably housed a bomb.

Jim had a perfect head shot, but what if he was right? And what if it wasn't just an M-80, but something big, kinetic, dangerous? A ZIF. The ripcord was tight enough that any inadvertent jerking motion might trigger the detonator.

The figure looked directly at Jim. He did not turn his weapon and he did not slow his determined pace toward the cafeteria.

It wasn't Karsten Nygard. Of course not. This boy was far too large, too wide, to be Karsten. This was a bodybuilder. This was an athlete.

This was Kevin White.

His face was utterly blank, his eyes unseeing yet somehow focused, a great white shark searching for its next meal.

Jim leveled his gun. "Stop there, Kevin! Stop!"

White didn't stop and his wooden stare didn't waver, but he released his grip on the rifle stock and released the ripcord from his teeth.

The bomb! Jim thought, scrambling backward. He rounded the corner into the south hallway and was stunned to see a half dozen teachers and a handful of students peeking out from partially open classroom doors. *Did you people not pay attention in the active shooter drills?*

"Go, go, go!" he yelled, his arms outstretched in a sweeping motion, herding them down the hallway to the fire doors. The alarm sounded as they burst outside into the unseasonable warmth, and Jim ushered them alongside the brick wall of the school, their faces full of blind fear. Some ran crouching. Some tripped over their feet, their bodies frozen rather than in flight, but Jim pushed them toward the front of the school.

The spray of semi-automatic fire sounded

again from inside, more frequently, as if the shooter had found his intended targets. Screams could be heard in the distance, and the *thock-thock-thock* of a Black Hawk circled the sky in his mind's eye, but he pushed it away.

"Move, move!" Jim cried. "Everybody stay down, get to the parking lot, and take cover!"

What is Kevin White doing with a backpack full of explosives? Jim wondered as he left them and crept back along the exterior of the building the way he'd come. White was failing chemistry; how had he managed to construct a bomb? He'd even been a victim, not the perpetrator. Unless he bombed his own truck? But why would he do that? Jim had to be wrong about what was in the backpack. After all, nothing had happened when White let go of the supposed ripcord. No, there was no reason to believe he was anything but a shooter.

Except an explosion had definitely gone off earlier in the east lobby. *Shit.*

Jim rounded the back corner of the building and squat-walked toward the steel emergency exit of the cafeteria. Just as he reached it, a blast of gunfire sounded from within and the door burst open, its siren unleashing as a student's bleeding body fell outside, his arms splayed above his head as his torso crashed down the cement steps. The door banged shut against his hips, pinning his blue-jeaned legs inside.

Through the gap, Jim saw Kevin White pivot on his heel, his quarry down, and turn his gaze back to the cafeteria. Blood was sprayed over the walls. It marbled the long cafeteria tables. Students were scattered across the floor. Some took cover under tables. Some lay dead in pools of their blood, just like Hot Patti.

Thock-thock-thock.

A news helicopter circled overhead. A Black Hawk circled overhead.

Jim smelled the blood. He heard the screams. Where was he? Where was K-Tell?

Thock-thock-thock.

Jim's eyes closed and he heard the choppers dusting on the pads just outside the OR tents at the FOB.

Thock-thock-thock.

He grabbed his end of the stretcher and raced from a Black Hawk to the triage flap while the occupant, a pale soldier with a puddle of blood where his leg should be, ogled Jim with the bald stare of death.

Thock-thock-thock.

More choppers circled, swirling the blood-spattered dirt deep into his nostrils. His tongue couldn't escape the coppery taste.

The images frightened open his eyes as they always did, but he still saw red. Portage red. Blood red.

But he also saw he had a clear shot at Kevin White, whose back was to him as he scanned the cafeteria for his next victim. This was Jim's chance to serve and protect, to earn his way out of SRO duty. He was an expert marksman, but even if he wasn't, this was an easy shot.

He tried to raise his gun, but his body didn't respond, as though his arm and brain were locked in a standoff. Doubts pecked at his bravery. He didn't have on body armor, just his measly blues. What if White went down spraying fire? What if there really was a ZIF strapped to his back?

Jim glanced over his shoulder to see if any sort of help had arrived, but the only sirens were from the fire alarms. He was still on his own.

Thock-thock-thock.

Time hung, like the Black Hawks loitering in the sweltering Iraq air. Death was meant to come from a low and stormy Middle East sky, not a bright Midwestern afternoon.

Jim was paralyzed with uncertainty, with fear.

Thock-thock-thock.

The state patrol helicopter arrived and began a tight circle. Next a Chicago ABC affiliate

helicopter appeared overhead. Now three helicopters loitered over the school grounds.

Thock-thock-thock.

Suddenly a flash of unexpected movement
caught Jim's attention. A red streak flew at
Kevin White, hitting him from his blind side,
low, at the knees. White twisted, crumpled,
and fell backward. A second student seized the
opportunity and jumped atop White's prone
body. Two more followed, pinning down his
legs. A sneakered toe kicked the hot rifle across
the linoleum.

The first tackler had been a girl. And not
any girl: Amber Parker. She wore her cropped
Portage cheer top and flouncy red and yellow
skirt, and her long blond hair hung in a braid.

She had tackled Kevin White and stopped
the killing.

While Jim Lord had cowered in safety just
outside the doors and done nothing.

* * *

Jim hadn't noticed the snap of the camera. The moment a photo was taken that would capture his weakest moment, a moment that would become infamous and synonymous with failure. With cowardice.

A parent had come to Portage High to take photographs at his daughter's basketball game. He carried his new Canon EOS 90D, a gift that Christmas. He was heading from the parking lot toward the field house when gunfire drew his attention to the main building and he saw a student tumble through the cafeteria's emergency doors, his shirt stained red. The father was relieved to see a uniformed cop at the door, armed and ready to go in after the shooter.

The officer knelt over the wounded teen and looked inside the cafeteria right as the father uncapped his lens, and focused. He clicked the shot at that exact moment when, crouched over a bleeding student, Jim had turned away from the crime scene, his eyes dilated with shock, his body frozen with fear, desperate for help. The result got the amateur photographer, just an Indiana dad in medical sales, nominated for a Pulitzer Prize.

It ran in every daily paper in the country. It ran in every daily paper in the *world*. The photo of the *coward*. The man who did *nothing* to save the school. The time the chicken-hearted and bumbling police officer hid behind a door while innocent children were killed.

Wave after wave of emergency vehicles poured into the bus lanes of Portage High School. Police arrived first and secured the area, quickly followed by tote-hauling EMTs, who grouped in twos and threes around the students lying in spreading pools of their own blood. Empty gurneys replaced full ones as quickly as they could be rolled in. A shock trauma helicopter from South Bend landed on the football practice field to evacuate two serious cases.

A thick line of police from various jurisdictions fought to keep the press and the public outside a hastily constructed perimeter. Within fifteen minutes, FBI from the Merrillville resident agency were on scene. Forensics officers snake-walked, photographing and picking up spent casings.

Through the open back door, police hustled Kevin White from the scene and into a waiting Portage County van. His wrists were cuffed behind his back and the trench coat was gone, but he still wore the same vacant expression. He also wore a black hoodie, and with a sickening feeling that sank deep into Jim's bones, he noticed the hoodie's black drawstring clenched between White's teeth.

Jim sat at the end of a cafeteria table nearest the steel exit doors. A cop he didn't know, from a force two counties over, stood silently near him. In time, a petite EMT squatted in front of him. The bottom of her heavy overcoat pooled around her. She shook Jim by both hands, searched his face, and looked into his eyes.

"Any blood? Are you hit anywhere?"

Jim knew her. They had met on a domestic call Jim had taken before he got sent to Iraq. She didn't recognize him now.

He shook his head no.

Police and FBI talked with students individually or in small groups. Jim couldn't see Amber Parker's face as she recounted her story to a man and woman in dark suits, but her braid swished along the back of her cheer uniform as she thrust her shoulder to the side and re-enacted the tackle from her seat.

Amber Parker, a real American hero.

Yet among the ironies and complications that would abound from the tragedy was the fact that she was perhaps also partially the reason for it. Amber and Kevin had dated briefly during freshman year, and she'd dumped him in the cruel way fourteen-year-olds can dump one another. He'd been hurt badly, in the way fourteen-year-olds can hurt. From then on, he had developed a menacing preoccupation. As she'd continued to find success both in and out of the classroom, he had not. It was his academic ineligibility for the coming wrestling season, the consequence of having failed chemistry, that created a dangerously unstable balance in his mind. When he invited her to the spring formal and she rejected him, the rebuke, combined with all his other issues, tipped him from being a heel into a killer.

Or so the court-appointed psychologist wrote in her evaluation. Kevin White didn't speak a word in his defense after being tackled in the cafeteria.

And neither did Jim. How could he explain that he'd mistakenly thought a hoodie drawstring was a bomb ripcord? That when he'd had a totally clear shot of the perpetrator, he'd been too chickenshit to take it? He couldn't explain it to himself, and he couldn't explain it to the world, because there was only one explanation: he was a coward and a failure. He was a poor excuse for a cop, a poor excuse for a soldier, and a poor excuse for a man.

The world didn't pin it all on Jim at first, of course. No, at first he was seen, like the rest, as a victim of the circumstances of another senseless school shooting. It didn't take long, though, as the grieving and the angry and the defensive all sought to cast blame, for Jim Lord, the armed SRO who watched as a cheerleader saved the day, to become the one who drew their fire. So Jim said nothing. There was nothing to say.

A firm hand clamped on his shoulder.

It was Uncle Jimmy.

"I've got him, I've got him," Uncle Jimmy

barked out to men around him. They were all wearing the mocha smocks of the county sheriff's office.

"Come on, Jim," he said in a quiet tone. "I got you. Just come with me."

5

Jim Lord descended into a hole so dark and deep and stifling that there was no real description for it.

Crash and splash didn't even come close.

Jim was in hell. Not hell with flames, pitchforks, and devils. And not the hell of a boundless void without the existence of God. Jim found himself in the hell that was a ferocious tumble through space. His body twisted at a rapid velocity. The spinning went on endlessly.

He lived in a cheap motel off I-94 at the Lake Station exchange. After the tragedy, his landlord had given him such a glowering look of censure and pity, Jim had slunk away from his shabbily furnished apartment in shame and landed in the first place he could afford. He couldn't even consider moving back in with his grandparents, who, while supportive, had a gleam of dismay in their eyes. They looked older. Aged. And it was his fault. So he gave them the only peace he could: He stayed away.

He woke every couple of hours to drink from the nearest bottle. Usually, it was vodka. Sometimes it was rum. He started most mornings by vomiting, then swished his mouth with water before taking another long swig of liquor and returning to his wrecked motel bed.

The traffic outside rumbled by, heavier in the morning and evening, but never quiet. In it he heard the choppers swooping in, their rotors beating, their racks jammed with dead and dying. On the back of his eyelids flashed the saucer eyes, the set mouth of death. Kerosene whipped at his nostrils.

He rarely ate. There was a Denny's next to

the Liquor Barn half a mile up Route 20, and sometimes he went in and ordered a stack of pancakes or a patty melt, but as often as not he couldn't eat what was put in front of him. His fork dangled limply in his hand as he sat in fear that he would be recognized as the coward whose inaction led to those kids being killed. He was like a time bomb, ready to detonate. Oh, the irony.

Mainly Jim slept. If he had enough vodka and rum, he could stay two days or more in his motel bed, moving only to pour another drink into one of the glasses he had stolen from the Denny's. The ice machine was only two doors down, but the cubes wouldn't last more than a few hours, so his bucket was usually half full of tepid water.

Sometimes he puked and nothing came out. Sometimes he'd wake to find patches of blood on the sheets, but no wounds on his body.

He dreamed of Iraq, of the awful carnage brought in by the Black Hawks.

Thock-thock-thock.

In his dreams, he carried a soldier hit by an IED while on patrol. Shrapnel had shredded the flesh on the man's legs and face, and blood sputtered around a chunk of metal lodged in his back. He screamed as Jim lugged him into the medic tent, until a medic rushed up and stuck him with morphine. Then Jim ran back out to do it again.

Thock-thock-thock.

While awake, he replayed the early television news broadcasts in his head.

A steroid-sick and mentally ill high school wrestler acting out after rejection from a popular cheerleader. The product of a culture of indulgence and special pleading. The result: seventeen students injured. Six students dead. Two teachers murdered. One administrator.

Among the dead: Karsten Nygard, junior.

Among the dead: Patti Triplett, school administrator.

Among the dead: Malinda Murch, chemistry teacher.

When his dreams weren't of Iraq, they were of Malinda. He didn't know which haunted him more.

For a few days, rumors swirled that the president would visit Portage High. He never did. Instead, Amber Parker went to the White House. The president gave her the Citizens Medal. She made a speech about bravery and the duty of humans to each other.

Often, when photographs of Amber appeared, they were paired with the one of Jim and the bleeding student, armed but useless, his eyes wide with fear as he pleaded with the world for help. Like a coward.

Coward. Had anyone not seen the

photograph? First were the late-night comics, making fun, smirking in the immediate aftermath at Jim's ridiculous impotency. Next the conservative news outlets and talk radio began harping on the shooting. The gun control lobby wondered why a nut like Kevin White had access to a rifle with the trigger restrictor drilled out. The NRA president went on a twenty-minute harangue in a building lobby in Reston, shouting until spittle formed on his lips that "had the officer on duty not been a *coward*, the situation would have ended with one death only, that of the gunman! He *did nothing* to protect the school!"

From that day forward, Jim's face—not his name, because people knew him mostly from the photograph showing his horror-stricken expression—became a byword for cowardice. He became a meme. He became a T-shirt.

His cell number got out somehow. Within a

day his voice mail was full with angry messages telling him to die. Eat it and die.

He couldn't really argue the sentiment.

Given the embarrassment of all involved—the school district, the Portage Police Department, and the Gary area in general—the wish had been for the scandal to go away as quickly and quietly as possible. Uncle Jimmy pulled all the strings he could for Jim to be dismissed honorably—a misnomer, admittedly, but it held some advantages—and Jim was set to be absolved of any civil liability. All he needed to do was sign a consent form with the Portage PD and walk away.

But Jim wouldn't. Not because he denied the facts of the matter. Not because he felt he had been treated unfairly. It was the opposite. Jim didn't believe he deserved to be brushed off gently, given an institutional break, and sent on his way with back wages from his suspension and the union-mandated settlement at termination. Jim wanted to be brought before the state law enforcement tribunal. Jim wanted to be found guilty.

And he was. For abdicating his police duty, his policing certification was revoked and he was prohibited from ever serving again in any licensed capacity in the state of Indiana.

Chuck Marlow was at the tribunal, the first time he'd seen Jim in weeks. He couldn't understand what motivated Jim. He could have resigned. It would have been done. His reputation and his character were already irreparably stained.

He wasn't the only one present. The story of the coward cop who let eight people die in the worst school shooting in Indiana history had packed the gallery with aggrieved parents. The press was also out in full.

There were a few notable absences.

Tom Harbaugh was not there. He had confessed to having left Portage High School early on the day of the shooting without proper permission or documented notification. He was fired from the Department of Natural Resources. He, his wife, and their infant son had moved to Florida, where his in-laws ran a motel in Venice.

Amber Parker was nowhere to be seen either, and Jim didn't know whether to feel relieved or disappointed.

Each week Jim paid cash at the semi-circular reception desk in the motel lobby. For some reason, it was important to his fog-choked mind that the counter was semi-circular.

One bleak, windy day—there was a hint of coming lake snow in the battleship gray clouds above; even Tom Harbaugh might have agreed it was cold—he needed cash to settle his motel bill. He walked through his hangover to the nearest ATM, while cars and trucks sped through the insistent Indiana cold. The freeway smelled of the salt they had spread during the last snow and that now coated every surface nearby.

Jim withdrew his limit at the ATM in a nearby truck stop. It was a lot of money to have on hand in that part of town.

Mug me, he thought, holding the cash in his hand. *Give me an excuse to kill. Give me an excuse to die.*

He stopped at the Durango Steak House next to the truck stop. At the bar he ordered a vodka grapefruit. The bartender teased him. She was pretty. He had another. For the first time since the shooting, Jim felt almost like himself. He felt good.

He ordered a steak and drank two pints of lager with it. He thought of asking the bartender, who wore a branded western shirt with pearl snaps and a name tag that said "Brice," for her number.

Afternoon shifted to evening and a new bartender came on.

He picked up Jim's tab and appeared to scoff.

At some point, Jim remembered having words with the bartender. Maybe it was the manager. They all looked the same.

He came to in the McDonald's parking lot. He had managed to order a coffee and sat on a white cement curb sipping it. Finally, a young kid in a striped shirt came out of the restaurant and politely asked him to move on.

The next Jim knew it was dawn. He was on his bed at the motel. His jeans had mud at the knees, and there was dried puke on his shirt collar and the right cuff.

He should have never been at that garbage high school on that garbage duty. Why did he have to be alone when the shooting started? Why didn't he take out Kevin White when he had the chance? Why did some smart aleck with a fancy camera have to take his picture as he crouched outside the cafeteria doors? Why?

Why did Jim need to play the coward for the whole world?

Only Chuck Marlow knew where Jim was hiding.

"Listen, Jim," Marlow had told him on one of the few calls Jim answered. "No one blames you."

"That's not true," Jim had replied. "The whole damn world blames me." *I blame me.*

"Please let me come down and chat with you," Marlow had insisted.

Jim, in his confusion and fear and doubt, not to mention his now perpetual drunkenness, could not properly discern Marlow's intentions. Others had reached out to him, too, but they'd wanted to shame him or attack him or make money off him, in one way or another.

Jim didn't want people. And that included

Marlow. Jim couldn't trust his judgment of anyone or anything anymore.

The haze was pierced one indistinct afternoon by a knock at Jim's motel room door. It was a raw spring day with a cold, mineral wind blowing straight off the frigid lake. Jim had been to the truck stop that morning, where he bought a plastic handle of Kamchatka vodka and ate a vending machine cinnamon bun. When he'd returned to his room, he'd crawled into bed and not moved since.

Jim figured it was Marlow, but in the gray glass light he couldn't make out the face of his caller, just that she was tall and slim and wore a blue quilted jacket with a corduroy collar. Her head was wrapped in a red silk scarf. "Hey, there, Jim," she said. "Do you mind if I come in?" She wrapped her index finger around the security chain and gave it a suggestive tug. Cold air shot from behind her into the room.

Jim tried to rub some comprehension into his face, but he was too drunk. He just knew there was a strange woman outside who knew his name.

He closed the door and slid back the chain, and when he opened it again, she eyed him with a hand on a jutted hip, then strutted past him into the room.

Befuddled, Jim followed her and sank onto the mattress while she took in the state of his affairs. Housekeeping had been by while he was scarfing down his cinnamon bun, so the room was not its usual wreck. The head-shaped impression on a pillow on the nearest of the two beds was all that differentiated the room from a freshly made one. That and the jug of cheap vodka, a third of its contents already gone.

Jim tried to focus as he perched on the edge of

the bed, but he still couldn't make out her features. As she unsnapped her jacket, it dawned on him she looked like Malinda.

"Why?" Jim asked.

"Friends sent me to you, Jim. Worried friends."

"I don't have any friends," he said.

"You do, Jim," the woman said. "You do."

She reached out her hand and Jim was hit with a fresh wave of drunkenness and nausea and toppled backward onto the bed. If he could close his eyes just a moment, perhaps all this would make sense.

When he opened them again, at some point deep in the night, he was sober enough to recognize it had all been a dream. He got up and took a piss, left his pants on the floor in the bathroom, and climbed between the sheets after downing the contents of a plastic tumbler of vodka he found on the nightstand.

As Jim closed his eyes, he could swear he heard a helicopter hovering outside. It inchwormed in, leveled, and dangled before the final touchdown. At dusting, the sound of the rotors changed, a combination of maximal surface compression and an easing of the throttle. In his mind's eye he saw the tall, dark-haired woman running toward the open door, half bent from the noise and the powerful downthrust of the blades. She stepped on the boot jack and vanished inside, then the pilot hit the throttle again, rotated, and the chopper began its tail-first lift. For a moment the front curve of the skids loitered. Then it was up and gone.

The chopper noise retreated, drowning alongside the blood and screams in the black water of his sleep.

Chuck Marlow continued to call regularly. Every third or fourth time, Jim would answer, but he refused all of Marlow's overtures to visit. Until eventually he caved.

He expected Marlow would give up any attempts to "help" him after seeing the pathetic mess he'd become, the squalor that surrounded him. But what Marlow found was a deeply downtrodden soldier in a cheap chain motel room with a few distinctly non-corporate touches. There was a calendar on the wall from the Wing Wah carry-out Chinese. A paper poppy drooped in a chipped white glass thrift store vase on the desk. An empty handle of rum filled the small garbage can.

Marlow's housewarming gift fit right in: a liter of Tennessee bourbon and two give-away liquor brand glasses that his buddy at the wine store down in Porter had dug out of the storeroom for him. Jim perked up when he pulled the bottle of whiskey out of the paper sack. It was a start.

Marlow rinsed the glasses in the small bathroom that smelled of motel soap. He poured two fingers and watched Jim drink. The first sip went down like fire and the second like a little bird. There was no question that Jim was on a glide path toward ethanol dependency.

"You ever get out of this place?" Marlow asked.

"Time to time," Jim said, tipping the mouth of his glass for another pour. It had a golden rim and a red advertisement for an Italian aperitif on it.

Marlow poured. "Think maybe you should get out more?"

Jim drank. He shut his eyes tightly, then opened them, rheumy and bloodshot. "Nah," he said after a moment. "What for?"

"See the world? Meet new people?"

"That's just cruel, Chuck. You know nobody wants anything to do with me."

"That's not true, Jim," Marlow said.

"Actually, there was one that came by." Jim rubbed his forehead, trying and failing to dredge up a clear picture of the woman. "Maybe it was a dream. She looked like Malinda. It must have been a dream. You're the only one knows where I'm at."

It took a while. Marlow came again the next week and then five days after that and then four. Each time he brought sour mash, though he knew that from a medical point of view it was undoubtedly the wrong thing to do. But it created a small opening, and with patience and time he was able to lift, little by little, the lid that rested so heavily on the coffin Jim had lain himself in.

One day when he thought Jim was finally ready, Marlow made his pitch.

"How about we take a trip?"

"Trip?" Jim asked. "Are you kidding me?"

"I'll rent a plane. We'll go for a fly."

"Me? In a plane?"

"You got the idea, Jim. You and me in an airplane. Get a little air. Get a little perspective."

Jim fell back onto his wrecked motel bed and turned onto his side.

Marlow had seen a lot in his life. He had seen men pushed to the brink of death. He had seen men as they slipped beyond it. This was a man teetering on that precipice. A man so depressed that, to the outside observer, death looked like a refuge.

When Marlow arrived the next day to pick him up, Jim looked slightly revived. He had been drinking, no doubt, but he was not drunk. Marlow had not brought the usual sack of Jack. He didn't enter the room. Instead, Jim followed him to his car.

Marlow drove west along I-90 to the exit for the Gary airport. He parked at the Coleman hangar and filed his flight plan. Jim tagged along as Marlow did the preflight inspection. His mood appeared to have lightened. He asked questions. He followed Marlow's hand as Marlow examined the flaps and ailerons and pitot-static tube. He crouched alongside him to examine the landing gear.

By the time they had lined up to wait at the end of Runway Two, Jim had nearly returned to his old self. He was animated. He cracked a joke. When the tower radioed clearance for takeoff, Marlow sensed Jim's bounding excitement. As the skidded gray tarmac fell beneath them, it was as if Jim had become a different person.

Their flight path took them nearly due north over Lake Michigan. Marlow adjusted direction so they could fly as close as practicable to the Chicago shoreline. As he kept them low, the buildings loomed massive: the Hancock Building, the towers of the Magnificent Mile. At the Wisconsin border, Marlow banked the Cessna left and took them over the shore. They crossed above Kenosha before turning again toward the south. Jim's mood remained elevated the entire hour-long flight. He was buoyant, talkative, and companionable.

Marlow was delighted by the change in his

friend as he brought the plane back to ground in Gary. But by the time he had finished bothering with the details of landing and looked across the cockpit at Jim, it was as if the lights had gone out again. Jim slumped in his seat. A dull and affectless expression had come across his face. Once again, he resembled nothing so much as a man facing execution at dawn. By the time they had taxied to the tie-down spot, any hint of post-flight afterglow had vanished. No adrenaline lingered.

But Marlow didn't give up.

The second time they flew together the same thing happened. Jim lightened up as they walked around the single-engine prop in pre-flight. While in the air, he returned to something approximating his old personality. And when they landed, so did Jim.

On the third flight, Jim asked to take the controls and Marlow said yes. Marlow wondered if he didn't have a death wish himself, giving the controls of a small plane over to a man who met fully the criteria for active ideation of suicide. But something told him it was worth the risk. Jim had not gone completely dark. There was enough of him left, the crescent moon of personality that had not been extinguished by his grief and shame, giving hope that a waxing motion might still occur.

They took half a dozen flights together, and each time Jim held the controls for an increasing amount of time. He had a natural athleticism and coordination. He had that sixth sense of direction that was unteachable. Either a person had it, like a migratory bird, or they didn't. Marlow sensed Jim had it.

On their last flight, rather than loitering around Chicago and its skyline, Marlow vectored them for Milwaukee. It was a beautiful early summer day, and a Canadian high bathed the lake and city below in brilliant light, the trees seeming to shimmer like wet emeralds while foxtail waved gently in the fields.

Marlow knew a great place for a brat. When they landed in Milwaukee, he watched Jim carefully. This time the touchdown did nothing to dampen the good mood. They took a cab to the East Side and had lunch at Von Trier. Jim loved it. On the flight back, Marlow took the Bojack route, to the west of Chicago. Jim spotted surprising things on the ground: the Elgin Watch factory and the Joliet Prison. For once, he did not recede entirely back into himself on landing at Gary International.

Hope was as rampant as the foxtail.

Marlow took a sip from his tumbler and gazed out the window at the menacing sky. He'd been right to call off the day's flight; the sketchy weather had gone dark, and potential wall clouds hung fat and black near the horizon.

The air crackled, the static and humidity mingling in a witch's brew.

He turned to Jim, who was sitting on the couch in Marlow's living room. "Not a good day to take to the skies," he said, right as the first burst of lightning exploded outside. A walloping crack sounded quickly after, and fat raindrops began to ping off the pavement. Awnings in the apartment complex flapped violently, and another flash lit the room, immediately followed by a massive rumble. In the distance, a tornado siren wound up.

Both men's cell phones beeped with an emergency warning. Somewhere out there, to the south most likely, sheared wind, bending its gray elephant trunk, was fixing to touch down.

Jim set down his glass for a refill, popped the cork from the whiskey, and poured: first a dribble and then a slop. Marlow was surprised to find Jim's expression as dark as the storm.

"You know what?" Jim said, his voice wild like the wind. "I hope someone brings it up. I hope someone, now that it's done and finished, I hope somebody, some yokel or redneck or, hell, housewife or punk getting gas, I hope they try to throw it in my face. Because I've stood there, before the world, and I've been judged. And the judgment was guilty. And the punishment I served in a moment and forever. Disgrace. But now that I'm cut off from job or honor ever again, no one, and I mean no one, can throw what happened at me again. I have served."

It had taken Marlow a moment to realize Jim was talking about the tribunal, a subject he hadn't brought up a single time on any of their flights. And now that he had, Marlow sensed an uncorked anger that he'd never heard from Jim before. Marlow had always expected Jim to be angry. Angry with Tom Harbaugh for leaving him at the school, angry at Kevin White for killing Malinda, angry at himself for not showing the bravery he'd thought he possessed.

But until that moment, Jim had shown only regret. Regret that the only life he'd known had been stripped away from him in a few stinging minutes.

"I've got to go," Jim said. "I don't know where. I know I'll never work as a cop again. I'll never work again, period. I'll never be able to find a job again, under my given name."

"Jim, you just need time."

"The world has turned completely against me, and I deserve it. I won't survive. I can't survive. I am cursed to a life without the ability to support myself." He choked and covered his face with his hands. "I'll never be able to redeem myself. I'm an exile. I'm an untouchable."

"The world is a big place," Marlow said.

"And there is no place in it where I can hide. I'm not a man. I'm a shadow. I'm a hunted animal."

Solemnly, Jim stood and shook Marlow's hand.

"But, Jim—" Marlow began.

Jim strode quickly to the door, opened it, and closed it behind himself.

Marlow waited. More sirens. More wind. His cell chirped with another emergency alert. A second tornado had just been reported touching down about halfway between Valparaiso and Wanatah. Cracks of thunder came steadily from the southeast, announced by electric flashes and tingling static.

After about twenty minutes, a knock came at Marlow's door. Jim was dry. He had been waiting outside the building under the eaves.

Marlow poured more whiskey into Jim's tumbler and pushed him gently back onto the couch.

"I can help you, you know," Marlow said. "I know lots of people. Helpful people."

Jim took another draft of whiskey. He'd had a good amount by then but showed no sign of drunkenness. His dark hair stood out some-how more defiantly on his head. His blue eyes burned bright. "I can't take your help," he said. "You know that."

"But why, Jim?" Marlow nearly pleaded. "Why be so bullheaded about it?"

"That's not it." Jim turned to look out the window, where the wind had picked up again. The second wave of the front, towering cumulonimbus clouds that had been feeding and growing mighty over Iowa and Illinois, now bumped to the ground like overloaded hot-air balloons. From their baskets rained destruction.

"You must let me help you," Marlow said finally. "I insist."

"You can't," Jim said. "I'm beyond help now."

Marlow wouldn't stand for it. "You're not, Jim. No one ever is."

"You've done what you could do, Chuck. Face it. Even good ol' Mr. Marlow can't fix this one. Don't get me wrong." He raised his hands in apology. "You've been a lot of help. It means a lot to me. You came to the inquest, didn't you? You were the only one. The only one!"

"But I can do more!" Marlow insisted. "I am doing more. I will do even more than you suspect."

"Oh," Jim said, his face twisting into a look of understanding. "Money." He shook his head. "No worries, Marlow. I've got enough for where I'm going."

Marlow ignored the apocalyptic slant of the comment. "It's not money I'm offering you, Jim." His tone turned to acid. "Get that thought out of your mind. It's pointless and superficial to your situation."

Jim looked startled, chastened. His cheeks reddened. "I'm sorry," he said quietly. "What a jerk I've been. Of course, you've helped me."

"I have," Marlow said, regretting the sharp thrust he'd made at a man who was, in every sense of the word, down.

"And, even if I don't know how or where or when, I trust you will help me again."

"That's correct," Marlow said.

Jim finished the whiskey in his glass and stood. "I should get going."

Outside, the front had passed. The sun shined on trees and grass a brilliant shade of green, as if they had just leafed out that moment.

"You know," Jim said, "I apologize for all the stuff I said."

Silence fell between them.

"You've given me confidence," he continued, standing strangely still. "I was going to say you've given me *back* confidence, but I realize . . . I realize now that I never had confidence. Not real confidence, the confidence that carries a man through adversity and challenge and loss. I never had that before. I was getting by on false self-esteem. I was a coward."

Again, silence.

"It's different now," Jim said. "I feel different."

Marlow noticed it then: Jim was standing tall, looking bigger and stronger than he had ever seen him.

"It's a strange feeling," Jim went on. "Freedom. A clean slate." His eyes lit up and he smiled at his friend. "That's it! A clean slate, that's what you've given me. I can go now. I can go and do and be free." He smiled and turned toward the door, as if he were off on an important errand.

"Wait." Marlow slipped around the corner into one of the bedrooms and came out with a handful of items. "Take these," he said, holding out a cheap pay-as-you-go cell phone and a heavy manila envelope.

Jim raised an eyebrow but accepted the parting gifts without hesitation. "Thank you, Chuck."

"Keep the cell phone charged. And good luck."

Jim nodded, and as he stepped through the

door, Marlow sensed a sureness in his gait, a confidence in his countenance. Like he could see the sun on the horizon after an interminable night.

Like there was hope.

6

Jim bought a used Toyota minivan, a family car for a man with no family. A suburban car for a man fleeing the suburbs forever. The back two rows folded flat and Jim could sleep on the length of them, with room for his duffel.

He pointed southwest and drove downstate all day, stopping at Shakamak State Park, west of Bloomington, where his grandfather had taken him one weekend when he was in high school. It rained the whole night, but the minivan did its job well and kept him dry.

The next day, which dawned clear and hot, he drove into Missouri. At dusk he pulled into

Montauk State Park, just east of Fort Leonard Wood. He was in the Ozarks now where he'd done his basic training. The heat and the humidity and the rolling prairie were all still familiar to him.

Jim stayed three nights at Montauk. Towering sycamores with peeling beige bark sheltered his camp space, which became a mental oasis, a place of safety where he tried to pinpoint the moment when things had gone so wrong.

Was it getting called up into the Reserves when he had just begun serving as a cop?

Was it getting assigned as a school resource officer in the first place?

Was it getting involved with Malinda Murch?

Jim took a swig of vodka and flat tonic water from his enameled cup—a Walmart special along with the folding camp chair on which he sat. The liquid was warm, but he didn't care enough to walk to the ice machine.

Jim pondered the name of the river flowing past the campground: the Current. The word rolled on his tongue, morphing from flow to philosophy. The Current River. As compared with the Previous River? As compared with the Next River?

He desperately needed to move on to the Next River. His sanity demanded it.

When he woke, he packed up his gear, such as it was, and policed the campsite. He packed his trash and walked it to the bear-proof dumpster behind the ranger station.

Ten hours later he pulled into the space he had been assigned at the Wichita Mountains Wildlife Refuge. He was finally in new terrain.

Jim lit his camp stove and put his Goodwill cast-iron skillet on the grate. He poured a small amount of vodka into the pan and swished it around until the blue flame below shot out yellow tendrils that reached the liquor. It blossomed in a cloud like the northern lights and went out. The pan was clean now, free of its thrift store taint.

Jim switched off the stove, and the blue flicker died. He left the skillet to cool on the burner. He wasn't hungry anymore.

He poured vodka into his enameled cup, fresh tonic this time, and sat in his blue camp chair and drank.

It was warm and misting when he awoke, groggily, the next morning. Jim packed up and went to see the nature preserve's renowned bison, following the map in a brochure from the ranger station.

From the designated viewing area, grassland reached toward a tall array of giant, reddish boulders, like the fossilized excrement of some extinct giant. Over them stretched a pale blue sky punctuated by a few perfect cartoon clouds. Bison clumped at the center of the diorama like living polka dots. Their shaggy shoulders hunched above thick beards and hard-curved horns.

A family in a minivan parked nearby. The father, tall and fit, crawled out first and stretched his back theatrically. Both rear doors began their slow slide open, releasing the noise of restive children. From one side spilled three kids, and from the other an older couple descended more slowly, resembling a magazine ad for Celebrex.

The last to emerge, from the passenger seat, was the mother, who took a look at herself in the mirror behind the sun visor before slapping it closed and climbing out.

Jim watched her. She wore her long hair combed straight and her western clothes looked genuine, not dime store or Ralph Lauren: roper boots and a pair of broken-in Wranglers, with a blue snap shirt open at the collar to show off a gold crucifix dangling from a gold chain at her throat and a red bandanna knotted around her neck. She followed her family up the short path to the observation area and stopped beside Jim.

"We're visiting down from Cherokee, Oklahoma," she said, as she raised her iPhone to the view. The phone was cosseted in the sort of protective case that came from outdoor stores. She snapped a few shots, then turned the phone horizontal and shot a couple more.

"It's been dry," Jim said. The pasture in which the bison roamed had run yellow with drought.

"It's always dry this time of year," she replied.

"You don't have bison in Cherokee?"

"If we did," she said, giving him a bright smile, "why would we be here?"

"Good point," Jim said. "No bison in Cherokee."

She smiled her long and bright smile. Jim looked toward her husband, who was barking at the children to crowd together for a photo with the majestic animals in the background. He wasn't having much luck getting them to converge long enough to snap a shot.

"Not much of a vacation, Wichita Falls," Jim offered.

"I don't mind." She narrowed her eyes at Jim. "I get mine in October when some girlfriends and I go over to Branson. Ladies' spa time and all that. Chateau at the Lake. You know Chateau at the Lake?"

Jim shook his head.

"It's a girls' trip, but, you know, a little cheese, a little wine . . ." She turned to look at the bison. "It can make a new person out of you," she added, almost to herself.

Jim couldn't imagine how she survived in Cherokee, Oklahoma. She was clearly an outsider, like him, she just hadn't yet been expelled.

The grandmother was staring at them.

"I'm Karen," the woman said and stuck out her hand. Jim shook it. "I keep horses in

Cherokee. Cherokee is famous for its equestrian trails. People bring their horses all the way from Chicago to ride there. Say it's the best riding in the whole country."

Jim smiled again and she smiled back.

"I'm from up near Chicago," he said.

"No kidding? Imagine that."

Jim looked once more in the direction of the husband, who hadn't seemed to have noticed him.

The breeze shifted suddenly. The scent of the dry grass and the dung and the bison themselves rose on the wind.

The grandmother, who stood at a distance not looking toward the bison, tugged on her husband's blue windbreaker. Obediently he tilted his ear to her mouth. She spoke barely three words before the man's head jerked up and he turned in Jim's direction.

No doubt the grandfather watched a lot of television. He probably watched a lot of Fox

News. Fox News had continued to fan hatred toward Jim. To Fox News, Jim and his cowardice represented everything wrong with the country under a Democratic president. To Fox News, Jim epitomized the spinelessness of a nation riddled with socialists. To Fox News, until everyone carried a gun, no one would be safe from the neglect of cowards like Jim Lord.

The old man barked toward his son, using the same volume and tone with which the son had barked at the children. The son, who had been squatting and pointing out the horns on the bulls, rose halfway from his crouch and swiveled his head. At his father's gestured summons, the son headed to where his parents stood near the car. He listened intently for a moment, then his head snapped toward Jim and he scowled. He quickly corralled the children back to the minivan.

The bison lowed in the pasture.

Jim looked back to Karen, who was oblivious

to the gaggle of nervous family waiting by the car as she leaned her hip against the tilted acrylic information panel.

"Karen!" the husband barked. "Now!"

The woman's face flashed to an expression of guilt. She glanced over her shoulder toward her husband. He made a big, sweeping get-over-here motion with his arm. Karen turned back to Jim and smiled a farewell before sauntering back to the minivan.

The father sped out from the parking lot, presumably eager to put distance between his family and Jim, sending gravel spitting from under the front tires as the vehicle climbed onto the tarmac of the road.

Clouds gathered as Jim watched the bison move slowly back and forth across the scenery. The wind shifted again, coming now from the northeast. For a moment, even in the heat, Jim thought he could smell fall.

* * *

Jim was too tired to drive on but too restless to stay put. The wind blew and the smell of early snow was in the air. The clocks had already flipped back. It got dark early.

Virgil's Lounge was a squat, adobe-colored tavern just outside Gallup, New Mexico, that advertised MEXICAN FOOD from the tall sign in the dusty parking lot. Jim was drinking among a group of pipeliners and deciding what to do next. The pipeliners' filthy white pickups were gathered in the parking lot out front. Each truck was jacked up and had aerials bent from the cab to the truck bed, with winches in front and neon orange flags hanging atop white whip poles. Pipelining was a big job there. All that natural gas.

The pipeliners' faces were windburned and grizzled. The Navajo among them, maybe a third of the men there, were heavy and wore their hair long. Everyone was drinking beer. Drained shot glasses dotted the bar, which was tended by an older gal with a frosted perm.

Nobody took much notice of Jim. He blended in, having been on the road for a while now. They knew he wasn't a pipeliner, because if you were a pipeliner in that part of the world you knew every other pipeliner working all the way to the Colorado line. But they didn't menace him either. Virgil's Lounge got its share of men drifting through.

In the way that working men do instinctively when they talk sports, they drew Jim into their haphazard huddle. More beer. Another round of Jim Beam shots.

Jim had heard that Native Americans couldn't drink. But these guys sure did and seemed none the worse for it.

All at once, the men in the bar were pulling on their jackets, buttoning, zipping. After having lounged without purpose for the better part of two hours, now they moved with dispatch. The group headed together toward the door.

"Hey, there," Jim asked the guy nearest him, a Navajo named Chester Clitso. "Where's everybody going?"

"Basketball," Chester said. "You can come if you want."

"Okay," Jim said. "Sure."

The man gestured to Jim to follow.

Chester led him to one of the pickups, distinguishable from the others mainly thanks to a bent antenna. He hopped into the driver's seat and helped Jim clear away clipboards and mysterious tools so Jim could ride shotgun. A laptop sat on a brace blooming out of the central console.

Chester bounced them onto Route 66. He drove fast and recklessly.

When he pulled into a large parking lot, Jim realized with a chill that it was at a high school.

The lot was crowded with trucks and other four-wheel drives, most of them coated with the same layers of dust, red in the sunlight but black like blood in the dark and cold, that covered Chester's rig.

The rest of the men gathered under an arc lamp, waiting. With Chester's arrival, they made their way through the cold toward the high school gym. Gallup High was to play its rival, Window Rock.

The gym was hot and crowded. The old-fashioned waxed-wood bleachers were packed, and yet more and more spectators entered and found seating.

The visiting team arrived on the court to raucous calling. The home team, in their red and black, emerged to heavy metal blasting from speakers that hung in the rafters.

Jim had never seen a game so fast and so intense. These weren't big, white farm boys with pimply arms and shoulders lumbering up and down the court. These were boys from the reservation, and they ran like hell.

The action moved hoop to hoop. There were crazy passes and wildly unlikely baskets, almost like in a Globetrotters game.

Gallup won.

"You want another like it?" Chester asked as he dropped Jim off in the neon-lit lot outside Virgil's after the game. "Chinle, where I live, they're playing Page. Big game tomorrow."

Jim climbed down from the truck. It was now bone cold in the wind, and the horn of the Amtrak Southern Chief headed for Los Angeles cut through the frozen air as it zipped past behind the restaurant.

"Sure," Jim said. "Why not."

"Four-thirty. Long drive out there. You can make it?"

"Sure," Jim said again. "Sure."

"Meet me here," Chester said, then pulled out into the night.

***

The sunset painted the entire and unimagin-
ably huge Western sky with the most intense
reds Jim had ever witnessed. And he'd had time
to take it all in slowly, as he spent forty-five
minutes waiting in the parking lot outside
Virgil's. He was now feeling ridiculous. With
each passing moment, he felt more self-con-
scious and alone.

Chester Clitso had probably forgotten
all about him and was halfway to Chinle by
now, if not there already. Why was Jim making a fool of himself? Why was he holding out
hope that anyone, once they knew him, would
come back?

Yet he waited. He didn't know why.

Finally, Chester's pickup veered off the highway with the same abandon as the night before. He took a long time to roll down the

window. Jim couldn't make out what he was doing in the cab. When the window did come down, Chester looked as if he had just been sitting there the entire time, a picture of pre-ternatural calm.

"That your vehicle?" Chester asked, nodding toward the minivan.

Jim nodded.

"Come on then, yo. Long drive. We'll go the short way."

Jim started the minivan and fell in behind Chester, who sped off, turning without looking across three lanes of traffic. They drove at first due north, fast and wild, before following the highway as it took an abrupt turn westward at Yah-ta-hey. After half an hour they hit Window Rock, on the Arizona line. Full darkness had fallen. The titular monument loomed in the darkness.

Chester took a hard turn northward, and Jim

did his best to keep up. After another half hour or so, Jim came up on Chester's truck idling in the middle of the road, which had begun to curve up into a low forest of mixed pinyon and juniper.

Chester was out of his truck, studying a red and white gate that had been swung across the road, closing it.

"Snow," Chester said, and Jim looked all around but couldn't see any. "Over there." Chester pointed into the distance.

"It looks closed."

"They want us to be slower," Chester said. "Maybe miss the game."

"How much snow, Chester?"

"A lot. They closed the gate."

Jim coughed. It had gotten noticeably colder. "Should we turn around?" he asked.

"Yi-yah," Chester said with a huff and a big blast of steam. He fussed with the latch on the gate and swung it open.

Jim got back into the minivan and followed him up the closed road. They wound up the side of a mesa, the pinyon beginning to give way to taller ponderosa. Still there was no snow on the ground.

It hit like an opaque shower curtain. The snow fell hard, and the road and the shoulder and the trees on either side were covered in white.

Chester drove no more slowly or carefully. When the road curved ahead of his truck, Jim could see that he broke fresh powder. This pass had been closed for a reason. Chester blew on ahead, the bed of his truck barely wavering, he had so much gear in it.

Jim did his best to follow, far enough behind that he would not be lost in Chester's spray but close enough to easily stay in the tracks of the truck. The minivan held up well enough, and Jim was not unfamiliar with driving in the soup. But combined with the winding road in a narrow canyon, this was of a different order of difficulty altogether. Chester gave no quarter.

Snow had piled rapidly on the branches of the pines the way it can only in the desert and at altitude. It hung there in huge clumps of white that glistened when the truck lights shone on it.

As soon as they reached the summit of this unnamed range, the snow ceased. Jim could make out a glimpse of lights twinkling in the grid of a small town in the distance. He followed Chester down the windward slope, which, more precipitous, forced even Chester to finally slow his pace.

The land flattened dramatically below. It was true red rock desert. The snow that had fallen remained only in daubs here and there. No trees grew. Even the creosote bushes were thinly spaced.

Once they came off the pass, the road straightened and was only wet. Chester, as if to make up for lost time, sped ahead. No cars came toward them. Jim was not certain what exactly he had put himself through. Still, he sent the minivan all out, trailing just behind the spray of Chester's tires.

Jim could not make out much of Chinle in the darkness, but they passed a Denny's and a Church's Chicken before coming up on a Best Western right before the intersection with what looked like a highway. Tucked back off the road was the brightly lit and clearly bustling Chinle High.

Chester parked across the road from the high school and Jim pulled in behind him. There was no room left in the campus lots. It was not as cold as it had been the night before in Window Rock, and Jim trotted to keep up with Chester who, despite his broad body and short legs, walked at an estimable pace toward the Chinle gym. They paid two dollars apiece and entered just as the first buzzer sounded.

The home team, the Wildcats, wore their

black and yellow and, after a hard-fought game with Page, won, much to Chester's satisfaction.

There was no discussion of the game afterward, or what would happen next. Chester just instructed Jim to follow, and they drove a short distance back up the road from the high school to the entrance gate of Canyon de Chelly National Monument. Chester paused and rolled down his window at the lit kiosk. The ranger was a white woman, a bit on the heavy side, stuffed into a light-gray ranger uniform. A thick blond braid hung down behind her ranger cap.

She said something to Chester, speaking Navajo. Chester replied.

He drove on. Jim followed, up a narrow road full of switchbacks.

"She's my brother's woman," Chester explained when they stopped at a pull-out in the dark.

"A white?" Jim had read that Navajo, more so

than any other native peoples, refused to marry outside their nation.

"Yeah. It happens," Chester said. "My grandmother, she was half-Spanish."

"How's her Navajo?" Jim asked. "The park ranger."

"Only so good."

They were stopped at a small compound on the north rim of the canyon. There was a low adobe-walled house, two trailers, and a shed.

"You can stay the night here," Chester said. "It's my mother's place."

"I can keep on," Jim said. "I don't want to impose."

"Everyone is sleeping," Chester said, as if that settled it. Inside, he handed Jim a heavy blanket and nodded to a sofa in the room just inside the front door. Then he disappeared down a darkened hall.

***

Jim awoke early to bustling sounds in the kitch-
en. He lay still on the sofa for a moment, not
disoriented exactly, but allowing the room to
come into focus in a way it had not been able
to the night before. A huge television screen
hung from the opposite wall and the room had
an overstuffed quality, with a lot of end tables
and brass figurines.

Jim slipped into his shoes and gingerly approached the small galley kitchen. At the stove
stood the white park ranger from the night before, cooking a pair of griddle cakes. A bag of
flour and a red tin of baking powder crowded
together on the small counter.

Jim didn't speak and neither did Chester's
sister-in-law. She wore gray twill trousers,
ranger boots, and a blouse with the park service
insignia in brown and green on the sleeve.

She finished by flipping the pancakes and

letting them turn golden on the other side, then slid them onto a heavy piece of stoneware. She handed the plate to Jim along with a fork. There was a small table with butter and a squeeze bottle of imitation maple syrup. She ladled two more griddle skidders into the pan.

When she joined him at the table, she introduced herself as Beth. Then she told him about her work.

"It's a good job overall," she said between bites. "But the schedule. It never stops. We're so understaffed. You do your time and, it seems like, everybody else's. People get sick. People go on vacation. People get transferred. People just disappear. Those of us got roots here, we pick up the slack. The national parks are broke. You can imagine the state of the national monuments. It's a shame, really." She broke off for a second to take another bite, then added, "Not surprised to see Chester. Basketball game?"

Jim nodded. He didn't know how to ask,

exactly, why she was there, cooking breakfast at Chester's mother's house. The pancakes were exceptional.

"It's all matriarchal, you know?" she said, as if reading Jim's mind. "If I were, I mean, under more normal circumstances, we would live with my people. But I don't have a family of my own. I mean, in Iowa I have a family, but you know."

"What do your people think of it?"

"They don't know what to make of it. They're farmers. It doesn't make any sense to them. I married a Navajo. To them it's like, somebody from Kansas, maybe, but an Indian? They're very practical people."

"Chester said his grandmother was half-Spanish."

"Navajo doesn't really have a past tense, at least the way it's commonly understood. When he's talking about his grandmother, who was *kidnapped* by Spaniards, by the way, which he does a lot, he's talking about an ancestral myth. There is a story in this clan about a woman abducted by conquistadors in the 1570s. She came back Catholic and pregnant."

"What about the cousin who's married to an Arapahoe?"

"Oh, that's real. That's Cousin Joe. Yeah, he's around. He married a girl he met over in New Mexico. I don't know how much Arapahoe she really is, but, whatever, she's not Navajo."

"How's your Navajo, by the way?"

"Better than a lot of Navajo," she said.

"Why is Chester living here?"

"He doesn't like his wife's people. He sees her a lot; they just don't live together. There's some beef between her clan and this one. Whatever. They're happy."

Chester emerged from outside, wearing a heavy jacket with a white synthetic shearling lining.

"You got something to eat?" he asked Jim.

"She made pancakes."

Chester nodded and said something to Beth in Navajo.

Out the window Jim could see an expanse of red rock desert, stretching far to the north. To the east ran a chain of snow-mottled peaks, through which snaked a ribbon of road, reflecting light. The land between was dun-colored and spotted with creosote. Twenty or thirty yards from the house, the pale pink sandstone gave way suddenly to the velvet gloom of the narrow valley below. Canyon de Chelly. The early sun had yet to strike there. The sky above was a violent blue, bluer than Jim had ever seen. Across the jagged chasm, the deep crimson rock of the opposite rim was stained vertically with desert tapestry in black and gray. The dusty green pinyon resumed farther on from the canyon edge.

"Come, Jim," Chester said, signaling with

his hand for Jim to follow him into the yard. He strode toward the canyon.

Jim could smell the cedar and dirt as Chester led him to a draw, into which they descended. It deepened quickly, the walls of sandstone rising over their heads. The trail was a journey backward through time. White Kayenta sandstone gave way to the rich vermilion sheen of the Wingate rock. Then, with no more than a step or two, they were into the Triassic and another gradation of red: The sloped, cardinal Chinle sandstone, named for that spot in which they stood, announced they were near the valley floor.

Around a sharp turn in the narrow slot canyon, Jim spotted the spindly profiles of cottonwoods, towering above the red sand. Tire tracks crossed the dry and curving streambeds where Navajo guides led jeep tours of the canyon. The valley floor was flat, scattered with the dead leaves of the cottonwoods. Willow-flecked seeps marked where water still managed to flow.

Chester nodded toward a cluster of cottonwoods across the valley floor that stood tall and bare against a bend in the opposite wall of the canyon. The morning light now caught the lip of the canyon and glowed a soft orange-pink. A small orchard stood near the grove of cottonwoods, and Chester walked in its direction. Jim followed.

Beyond a collapsed shed, its tilted walls weathered gray, Chester kicked with a boot at the bough of an apple tree lying on the ground. It appeared to have been torn from one of the trees in the orchard. The ground around it was scattered with gnawed apples.

"Bear," Chester said, as he poked with a stick at a big, black pile of scat. He pulled two apples from higher branches of the offended tree and handed one to Jim.

Chester stepped into the doorframe of the roofless shed. Two sidewalls and the back, made of ancient-looking adobe bricks, were intact, though the plaster had mostly eroded. Of the front wall, only the short section from the side to the doorframe still stood, on a shallow foundation.

"I was little here," he said.

"You grew up here?" Jim asked.

"I did. Here. In here."

Jim looked around. A disused and rusting cast-iron Franklin stove stood in a corner. There was no floor.

The space could not have been larger than ten feet by twelve. No electricity, no running water.

"I used to sit there," Chester said, pointing to a corner. "Playing while my granny cooked."

"Good food?"

"Good," he said. "Stew and bread. Good bread."

The sun rose over them. The day was clear

and warm. They stood in the silence and munched their apples.

Give us our daily bread.

"Was this your mother's place or your father's?"

Chester seemed to think for a long time. He took a perfunctory final bite from his apple, then threw the core off into the tall grass beyond the ruined house. "My father's people. This place still belongs to my father's people."

"You like it down here?" Jim asked. "Here and up on the mesa? At your mother's place?"

"It's where I'm at," Chester said.

Those words rang in Jim's ears like an echo in the canyon, and sank as deep into his soul as he'd sunk into the earth's layers on their descent. *It's where I'm at,* he repeated in his own head. And he knew it was time to move on.

Back at the main house, Jim thanked Chester for everything. He was long past the point of wondering whether Chester knew or how much. Chester always seemed to know.

"You're pretty good for a white man," Chester said and clapped Jim on the shoulder. It was a gesture out of a Western movie, but from Chester it felt somehow genuine.

Jim climbed into the dusty minivan, started it, and backed out onto the dirt road.

7

After leaving Chester Clitso, Jim drove south. When he hit the Mexican border, he decided to call Chuck Marlow. If one person should know where he was, Jim figured, it was Marlow.

He retrieved the cell phone Marlow had given him and studied the manila envelope that had been tucked into his duffel next to it. He pulled it out and felt its bulk, then opened it for the first time. His pride hadn't allowed him to prior. He wasn't surprised to find a thick stack of cash, and was only half surprised to learn the heft had come from a 9mm Beretta.

But there was something else in the envelope, too—a gold ring inset with a jade stone.

"Huh," he murmured as he slipped it onto his right ring finger and held his hand up to examine his new look. There was something carved into the jade, he realized, an animal of some kind. He squinted and brought the ring closer. Was it a cougar?

He thought about asking Marlow to explain, but in the end opted against it, figuring he'd just get a tall tale that needed deciphering. But he had to tell him something anyway, so he pulled up his number, the only one programmed into the phone, and called. Marlow answered on the first ring.

"I'm going down into Mexico," Jim said. "I thought to tell you."

"I'm glad, Jim," Marlow said. "How have you been?"

"Getting better, bit by bit."

"Good man," Marlow said. "You ready for a suggestion?"

"Maybe. Not now, though. Maybe later."

"Keep driving, Jim," Marlow said. "Get to Guadalajara and call me again."

"Okay," Jim said. "I will." He hadn't had a particular destination in mind before, so Guadalajara it was.

Jim didn't rush. He wasn't certain yet that he was ready to accept Marlow's help. He didn't even know what sort of help Marlow could offer, and he didn't want to raise his own expectations. He wanted to stand on his own feet.

After a few days in the minivan, he found his wanderlust beginning to flag. The time with Chester, short as it was, had changed him. Jim had no intentions of going back to Indiana, but he was done running as well.

"I've got an old friend," Marlow said when Jim called after checking into an interesting old hotel near the center of Guadalajara.

It was inexpensive, as was everything around there, he was learning. He was surrounded by tourists, rolling their own cigarettes and drinking Mexican beer. "He's offered to give you a situation."

"A situation?" Jim asked.

"A position."

"Okay," Jim said. "Here? In Guadalajara?"

Marlow laughed. "No, not there. It's a good piece from there. Somewhere well off the usual tracks. A place for someone to get away for a time. Time to think."

"I could use some of that," Jim said. "And a little anonymity."

"You'll be anonymous, I assure you," Marlow said. "This place is as tight-lipped as a Nar-Anon meeting for doctors and nurses."

"I see," Jim said. He didn't, but he knew to roll with Marlow's riddles.

Marlow gave him the name of a town. He was to get there as quickly as he could and he'd be

working at a resort, doing whatever was needed. "Keep to yourself, do your best, and good
things will come," Marlow said. "Good luck."

Jim allowed himself one tourist stop, in
Mexico City, to see the National Museum of
Anthropology. The jade and the gold and the
gods and the feathers mystified him. He wondered what it would be like to travel to that
time. To have a chance to prove himself in a
world so elemental.

From there he made his way first to Veracruz
and then on to Campeche. In Mérida, the
Toyota minivan huffed to a halt and never started again. Jim sold it for a few thousand pesos
to a scrap dealer.

A mistake at the bus station sent him to Tulum
rather than Chetumal as he had intended, and
a couple of further misadventures landed him
in an abandoned cruise-ship stop called The
Lost Kingdom. There were no cruise ships in
port, nor any other boats, for that matter. After

asking around, two men sitting on a bench in the shade of a tiny open mercado, little more than a corrugated metal shed roof over a handful of stalls, told him he could hire a boat. It was the only way to get where he was going without retracing his steps nearly to Mérida.

Jim spent the night in his sleeping bag on a bench in the abandoned cruise-ship terminal. The facility looked as if it had barely been used. The thousand-foot cement-topped pier stretched into the inky darkness of the tropical night, and a single arc lamp burned at the end. Jim fixed his eyes on that point before falling asleep.

Early the next morning a gaily painted skiff tied off at the pier head. A man in a grease-smeared T-shirt and a battered fishing cap called to Jim from the stern.

"You the gringo wants to go down to the fancy place?" he asked.

"Fancy place?"

"You know, the place where the pretty girls all go, and the movie star honchos."

Jim thought for a moment. To begin, he had not asked for a boat yet. The men at the mercado had told him to return there early in the morning, suggesting one of the men who had come to sell their catch might be persuaded, with hard dollars, to run him south.

The morning sun had barely crested the horizon, but the coral pink sky had dissipated quickly. It was now Wedgwood blue.

"Maybe there's a mistake?" Jim said tentatively. "I'm headed to a little fishing village down the coast." He needed to glance at his pocket notebook to even remember the name. "Altún," he said.

"*Sí, sí,*" the man said. "Altún, *claro.* Let's go, amigo, I want to be back in time for my dinner!"

Jim handed down his duffel and hopped awkwardly into the front of the boat.

"Sit here, closer to me, señor," the man said.

"Oh, and the monies?" He held up two fingers. Jim paid from the thick fold of cash he carried closely.

The man pushed off from a fat cement piling, settled on the bench in the stern, and turned the bow a half circle. With a quick rotation of his wrist, he powered up the big Mercury outboard. The skiff shot up and out into the rising sun.

Two hours later, after brief introductions but not much other conversation, Mauricio curved the boat hard starboard into the coast. Palm thickets lined a long stretch of white beaches and quiet mangroves. Soon Jim saw what had to be their destination. An impressive step pyramid belied the area's Maya history, and a mottled white and gray tower, its four square tiers stacked like a wedding cake made of stone, rose even higher beside it.

As Mauricio throttled down and guided the skiff through a gap in the reef, Jim began to make out the nearby village, which appeared to be little more than a series of huts lining a single street that ran parallel to the beach, well above the high-tide mark. Behind the village, Jim spotted the belfry of a whitewashed chapel.

At the north end, a dilapidated palisade fence enclosed a compound of some sort. A pier jutted out, and as they drew closer, Jim could see that the ruins complex was larger than he had at first thought. The tower perched on a promontory at one end, and the remainder of the grounds featured a second step pyramid, a colonnaded building, and another structure Jim couldn't quite figure out. There was no roof and one end was open, so you could walk right into a courtyard of sorts that was lined with steep walls. Or maybe it was a ball court, Jim thought, noticing it had two small vertical hoops on the walls and remembering how the Maya had played a strange basketball-like game—didn't it involve ritual slaughter? He'd have to look that up sometime. An emerald green lawn ran between and around the ruins.

Farther up the shore still, he picked out what must have been the resort where Marlow had found him a position. A long, limestone wall with terracotta coping separated it from the ruins complex. From behind it poked steeply sloped thatched roofs, crowded by a thick oasis of palm trees. The rake of the gray roofs and the profusion of green palms, surrounded by a perfectly straight white wall, gave the overall impression of incredible wealth.

Two men stood at the head of the modest village pier. One looked Mexican, like Mauricio, but the other was less identifiable, perhaps European. He was round and short, and wearing a tattered linen suit.

Mauricio pulled the skiff even with the low pier. Jim hoisted his duffel onto the dock and climbed out after it. It seemed that the Mexican nodded to Mauricio, who gave a whistle. Jim turned toward him.

"*Adios, amigo!*" Mauricio cried, waving his hat goodbye. "*Buena suerte, mi amigo!*" He twisted the throttle, shooting the boat for the pass in the barrier.

"*Bienvenidos*, Señor Lord," said the awaiting Mexican, much to Jim's surprise. Until two hours ago even Jim hadn't known he was coming via skiff to this village, so how did this man know his name? "I'm Héctor," the man added. "We have a good friend in common. The marvelous Señor Marlow. You know, yes?"

"I don't," Jim said in confusion. "I mean, I do, yes, Chuck Marlow."

"Don Carlos," said the man. "*Estimable* Don Carlos."

"Héctor!" barked the little round man in the ratty suit. His bald head was an evenly tanned nut brown. Besides the comically stained and wrinkled summer suit, he carried a bamboo cane and a Panama hat with a broken brim.

Héctor looked pained. "This man is Cornelius O'Connor," he said. "He is the man you *replace*."

"How do you do," said the man, jutting out a similarly deep brown hand for shaking. He wore a pair of European-style loafers on his feet and no socks. The loafers looked shiny with palm oil.

Jim shook hands with him.

"I am, as he says, your predecessor as the station chief of El Altún," he said.

He spoke English well enough, Jim thought, but with an absurd affectation. "I guess I didn't realize," Jim said, "that you retired, I guess."

"*Ahem!*" Cornelius said, clearing his throat and bringing a huge handkerchief, wrinkled and stained yellow, to his mouth.

The three men walked a short distance down the red earth path that led to the palisaded compound. Cornelius gestured them through a wrought-iron gate that was rusted open. A dirt yard with occasional tufts of sea grape baked in the already oppressive sun. The surrounding limestone walls were vine choked and crumbling.

At the center of the compound, a single-story house stood on pilings sunken into the limestone substrate. A wraparound veranda lined the square structure, which was topped with a raised-seam tin roof that had likely once been painted red but had faded to pink and was peeling on the windward side. Six gaily painted wooden steps led upward from the dusty yard to the shade-protected porch.

Two other buildings in varying states of deterioration lay to the jungle side of the house. Compared with the splendor of the resort a short distance away, this place looked as if it had been nearly forsaken to the inevitable climate-induced decay.

Cornelius explained that the station had been the headquarters of a long-since-abandoned palm-oil plantation. A Belgian consortium established it at some point in the forgotten past. It had never amounted to anything; the cannery had never even processed any raw palm oil.

He led Jim on a quick tour of the dilapidated buildings. Though its roof remained intact, half the floorboards in the warehouse had rotted through, and Jim could see a jagged layer of ancient coral in the dark below. Only a roof and two walls remained of the second building, which had been the cannery. Nearby, a shovel was frozen in the center of a small, motorized cement-mixing drum.

Next, Cornelius led them up the steps to the veranda of the house. The heavy front door, painted blue like the steps, was open behind a screen door.

"Señor," Cornelius said to Jim, opening the

screen for him, "please place your grip inside. The room immediately to the right will be yours. It is the finest."

Jim set his duffel on the floor of a cool and darkened room. A woven hammock hung from the beams, and a woven mat lay on the otherwise bare plank floor. A crucifix was mounted on the wall above the hammock.

Jim joined Cornelius and Héctor back in the courtyard, where an unusually small and hairless twig of a man sidled up to Cornelius. He wore only a rag at his waist. It looked like a diaper. He was serving Cornelius coffee in a broken-handled mug from a bamboo tray.

"You fool!" Cornelius yelled to the tiny, leather-skinned man. "Can you not see I have a guest? Careless insolence!" He raised a hand as if to strike. "Bring Señor Lord a coffee! Immediately!"

"*Sí, sí, mi jefe!*"

Cornelius snatched the mug before his servant scampered off and took an imperious sip.

Soon the small man—an imp almost, Jim thought, tanned as deeply as his master but of a strange and shriveled physiognomy—returned with a second chipped mug filled with coffee and cream. He carried nothing for Héctor.

"He's a bad guy, boss," Héctor Yañez said later when he and Jim were alone on the veranda at the house. "But he's got no teeth. He's just an old lady who gossips and moans."

Héctor's gaze suddenly dropped to Jim's hand, which was resting on the table and still wore the jade ring Marlow had given him. Jim noticed a flicker of recognition cross his eyes, then Héctor looked back up and continued. "Later on, I'll bring you to the big boss, Yax Pakal. He is the main man here. He is the chief, *batab*, of all the people around."

Jim nodded distractedly, more interested in his current situation. "This guy, Cornelius, he's the man I'm replacing?"

Héctor equivocated with his shoulders. "He was big boss of this station, once. But nothing has happened at the station for a long time." He nodded in the direction of the resort, which was barely visible between the old Maya tower and pyramid. Jim could see a thatched roof-top peeking out between closely packed palm fronds and banana leaves dancing in the breeze. "Over there is Las Posadas; a nice guy runs it. Called Antonio. He's from up north but not a bad guy. When the hotel started getting big, this guy, Antonio, he came out to run things. After that, Cornelius stopped doing anything. What did he care? The money still came."

"They let him stay on? The owners?"

Again, Héctor shrugged. "He stayed. Whether they know or care, I don't know. He drinks Presidente brandy all day. He's gotten a little . . ." Héctor held his hand out level and wobbled it. "People don't like him around their children. The little girls, though, they don't need bother."

"Do you work at the hotel, Héctor?" Jim asked.

"Oh, sure. You'll see me down there all the time, sometimes with my son, Sammy. I take the gringos out when they want to fish. But they don't fish much anymore. They come, do their thing with the colored blankets on the beach. They listen to an old lady ring a bell and they hum. That kind of thing. No so much fishing anymore. But some of the ladies, señor." Héctor flicked his hand, making a loud snapping noise between his forefinger and thumb.

"So, you do work at the hotel, then."

"I do lots of things, señor."

Jim couldn't tell how old Héctor was. Salty Panama hat, old khakis rolled up his strong calves, a once-white dress shirt now buttoned only at the waist. He was deeply tanned and wrinkled from a lifetime in the coastal sun. When he smiled, his canines were edged in gold. But he wasn't a menacing sort. His eyes were kind. His wiry build suggested he could handle himself.

"And, *pues*," Héctor continued. "Like I say. Pay no attention to the *gordo*. The *borracho*. He is nothing but an old lady."

A big grin suddenly spread across Héctor's face, and Jim turned to see a plump woman laden with a large platter and a jug amble onto the veranda. She wore a colorful frock and an apron encircled her ample waist, but what Jim noticed most were her kind eyes and the warmth she exuded, like a mother and grand-mother and favorite aunt all rolled up in one.

"Abarrane!" Héctor called, gesturing her clos-er. "Meet our new station chief, Jim Lord. Señor, this lady's going to fill your belly like no other! Her tortillas are fresher than fresh, and look at this plate of fish. My mouth is watering, boss!"

Abarrane gave Héctor a playful grin, then bowed her head slightly at Jim as she set his meal on a table positioned near the rail but safely within the shade of the veranda roof. She nodded a farewell before backing away and leaving Jim with a feast of fresh seafood.

"Enjoy, señor," Héctor said and licked his lips, then he left Jim with the promise to return for him early the next morning.

Jim ate his meal in silent appreciation, suitably impressed by the flavors and textures and thankful that Cornelius and his dwarf helper were nowhere to be seen. Sated, he went to his hammock and read, a battered copy of Conrad's *Chance* that he'd stumbled upon in a charity shop in Tucson.

As the swift, subtropical dusk gathered, Jim glimpsed a sepulchral shadow cross the courtyard. He thought he saw the shape pause at the door of the house and turn toward him, but in the gloaming, he could not be certain.

It was the figure of a woman, that much he could tell. She filled him with a strange sense of déjà vu. Her figure was slim and dark, and she wore a scarf over her head, a bright red one, Jim thought, though he had no idea how he could make out the color in the waning light. The breeze as it blew inland caught the wings of her kerchief and made them dance. She floated, or so it seemed, back down the steps from the veranda and into the yard. Again she paused, looking toward Jim. And then she just vanished, like an extinguished light, into the darkness ahead.

Her presence unnerved Jim, as if it bore him a message. She stirred a feeling in him that had been long dormant, perhaps even dead, since the afternoon when his life, as he had known it, ended.

Jim was not as a rule superstitious, but he had sensed something in that figure. Something eerie, yet familiar. The red scarf, the movement, the way she was gone in an instant. It reminded him too fully of Malinda Murch, and it jogged a grainy memory from his drunken stint at the motel. He didn't go in for ghosts or visions, but he couldn't ignore the tingle crawling up his spine.

For the next week, and then the next month, Jim would attempt to be at the station house as near that same time as possible, hoping that he might catch sight of the figure again. But she didn't reappear.

As promised, Héctor met Jim at the station house the next morning. Jim was nervous as they walked to meet Antonio, the director of Las Posadas de Altún, and all he registered of the resort was a blur of thatched roofs and whitewashed walls.

"This is the one who knows Señor Klopp?" Antonio asked Héctor, barely looking up.

"No, no. He was sent by a friend of Don Javier. The friend is a good man. A man I have known almost as long as I've known Don Javier himself."

Antonio shrugged. In this world, everyone was "someone" and every someone knew another someone who had a bigger name still. In five years, Antonio had seen them all. No longer starstruck, his favorite day was when a reservation crossed his desk not with a long list of "non-negotiables" but rather the simple notation "Wants to be left alone."

"You ever tend a bar?" he asked Jim.

"No," Jim said.

Antonio looked at him over reading glasses that sat low on his nose.

Jim recalled what Marlow had told him over the phone. He was to do whatever was asked of him. "I mean, yes, sure, I tend bar. I'm good." Sometimes bluffing was the better strategy, Jim had learned in the Army.

"Good. I just fired my last bartender this morning. Héctor, could you take Señor Lord and introduce him to the Bar Balché? I'd like him to begin with the cocktails this afternoon."

Jim followed Héctor from the reception area to another thatched-roof building, which turned out to be the bar. With its peaked roof and open-air plan, the Bar Balché looked exactly how Jim thought a tropical bar should look. Especially the wall of fancy liquor bottles, which he now stared at in befuddlement.

"You really know how to tend bar?" Héctor asked.

"Not a thing," Jim said, smiling.

"So I figured." Héctor laughed boisterously. "Here, let me show you a few of the most popular drinks."

Héctor gave Jim a crash course in liquor and wine, in sweet vermouth and dry, and on the difference between aperitif and digestif. Blended, unblended, peaty, or smooth? Barley or rye?

Dutch or English? The number and style of tequilas alone boggled Jim's mind. He faked his way through the rums. His approach toward making cocktails was largely intuitive, aided by a very general crib sheet, written in poor Spanish, left behind the bar by the last keep.

As Jim mixed his first mai tai, Héctor cheered him on. Jim waited nervously while Héctor took a sip. He swished the liquid around in his mouth for a moment, appraising the flavor, but giving nothing away. Then he grinned and patted Jim enthusiastically on the shoulder. "Well done, señor!" Then he gave Jim a tip that proved lifesaving in the coming months: "When in doubt, just pour more of whatever's the most expensive."

It turned out that was more or less the catch phrase for Las Posadas: "Too much of the best of everything." And even though Jim was just a bartender, he got a little taste of the motto himself.

At Héctor's invitation, in the early afternoons, before the guests of Las Posadas were
served the large meal of the day, Jim joined the
other workers at the rough-hewn table in the
kitchen for a *comida* of their own. Over his first
weeks, the resort staff took pride in guiding
him through the remarkable—and remarkably
strange to Jim—Yucatecan dishes they preferred. Maria Itzél, the head cook, a stout and
forever smiling Maya woman, stood by happily
as Jim was introduced to poc chuc, sour oranges, and pumpkin seeds.

He was starting to feel like one of the crew.
He was starting to feel a new sense of home.

Despite the ghostly vision glimpsed the first
night, the only inhabitants of the station house
besides Jim were Cornelius O'Connor; his pe-
culiar servant, whom Jim learned was called
P'en; and Abarrane, the Maya woman who not

only cooked, but also cleaned. Jim rarely saw Cornelius. As best he could tell, the man spent his days swinging in the hammock in his darkened room, attended to by P'en, who refilled his glass of rum whenever it was empty. On the rare occasions when Jim and Cornelius encountered one another, Cornelius would pause and bow deeply. The act was overdone and sarcastic and annoyed Jim and always made him wonder why he still hung around.

He understood Cornelius felt supplanted. But Jim found the resentment ridiculous. Cornelius had been in Altún for years. Jim had been there only a few weeks.

One day after breakfast, Jim decided to talk to Cornelius in hopes of clearing the air. He made his way down the darkened hallway at the back of the station house toward Cornelius's room. P'en always kept the shutters closed on that side of the house. When Jim reached Cornelius's open door, it was dark inside. He paused for a moment, deciding whether to knock on the frame or simply save it for another time.

Before he had chosen, a hiss came from the darkness. It was loud and violent, an animal noise, like the spitting of an angry cat. Suddenly, P'en's small, round face appeared out of the humid gloom. His eyes were wide, and his features twisted in anger. He opened his mouth, baring rotted and pointy teeth, and hissed again.

Jim recoiled in surprise and retreated along the corridor. He glanced over his shoulder once, but the sound had stopped and there was no sign of P'en having followed him from the room.

He emerged into the morning sunshine on the veranda and shook off the creepiness of the encounter. He didn't know what that was all about, but his talk with Cornelius could wait for another day. Or forever.

Later in the week, he asked Héctor for the

story behind those two bizarre men. And it was quite a tale.

Cornelius O'Connor had arrived in Altún from British Honduras, carrying a letter from the headquarters of Grupo Klopp, a hospitality company based out of Monterrey, about thirteen hundred miles away in the northern Mexico state of Nuevo León. In those days, there was only the village, the Maya ruins, and the remains of the abandoned palm plantation. The letter, signed by company president Javier Klopp himself, stated that the palm plantation and the surrounding land for a great distance, including the lime and coral on which sat the little village of Altún, now belonged to the Klopp company. It further stated that Cornelius O'Connor was to be the company representative effective immediately. Other developments were to come. More information would follow.

Cornelius installed himself in the station

house and immediately set about acting impe-
riously and alienating every being near and far.
He expected the villagers to work as his servants, for free. He owned their land, didn't he?
Their service would serve as rent.

He claimed to be the *alcalde* of the town and
treated everyone with scorn and condescen-
sion. The villagers of Altún were simple people
of faith, mostly of Maya descent. They were
accustomed to serving their authority figures—
the priest who visited and the local *batab*, Yax
Pakal—but even for these gentle people there
were limits. Cornelius made unreasonable and
inequitable demands of their time, labor, and
fealty. There were other and darker indignities
rumored as well. When he began to cast his
beady eyes over the youth of the village, the
alarm went out.

After a few months, Yax Pakal, a figure who
was a blend of Maya priest, princeling, and
strongman, decided to take action. In ancient

times, he would have dispatched warriors gird-
ed in armor, clad in jaguar pelts, their helmets
fiercely plumed with brightly colored feathers.
In the modern age, the warriors were five men
in a small, red pickup truck. The intention was
the same: to seize Cornelius, bind him, carry
him deep into the jungle, and deal with him in
the ancient way for prisoners and traitors. His
heart would be taken from his chest while still
beating. His carcass would be left for the coati
and king vultures.

Just before the warrior party was to act, a massive convoy of trucks snaked toward the village,
casting up a giant cloud of dust and exhaust.
In their bays they carried building materials,
heavy equipment, and men. The construction
of Las Posadas began. Every man, woman, and
child in the village was given meaningful work
and good pay.

Cornelius barely escaped with his life, whether he knew it or not. His brief reign of terror

ended as quickly as it had begun, and he was returned to being a figurehead at the station, with no sway beyond the compound gates.

After a time, two other outsiders arrived at the station house. One was a beautiful woman, her pregnancy just beginning to show. The second was a dwarfish man of uncertain ancestry who served as Cornelius's valet.

The woman was said to be Cornelius's wife, though Abarrane, then a young woman herself early on in her role as the station's cook and housekeeper, said they did none of the things expected of a husband and wife. Many months later, the woman had her baby, a girl. The following Sunday, she took the infant to the Chapel of San Torcuato, where the circuit priest baptized the child. Two weeks later, the mother was dead.

A black hearse arrived, sent by Grupo Klopp. The mother's body was taken back to wherever it was from which she had come. A legend arose among the villagers that the long, black vehicle, so foreign to their eyes, was a chariot of the gods and had taken the deceased woman directly to heaven.

Cornelius took no interest in the child whatsoever. It was Abarrane who, with the help of other village women, raised the little girl. When she was old enough, she was sent away to schools, Catholic institutions, mainly, from which she was forever being expelled. On holidays or between terms—or between schools, as was often the case—the girl would return to Altún and the station house, to be cared for by the cook and villagers. They called her Jewel. Whether that was her Christian name or a term of affection, no one knew.

And so passed the years. Cornelius O'Connor was largely forgotten. He rarely left the station house compound. His food and rum were delivered monthly, as part of his compensation,

the reason for which long forgotten, as he himself seemed to be, from the Klopp company.

To celebrate the first month of Jim's employ-
ment at Las Posadas, Héctor took him fishing.

He kept his personal fishing skiff in the mangroves beyond the resort. The hull was bright
blue and the gunwales international orange.
An old but robust Mercury outboard powered
it. Héctor pulled off the old canvas covering
and retrieved a tackle box and a jerry can of
gasoline from the ramshackle shed nearby.

After some coaxing, the outboard started,
and Héctor nosed the skiff through the man-
grove shallows toward a passage that opened
into the village inlet. He pointed them toward
the reef, slowing only to make certain he had
found the correct gap in the shallow coral. Clear,
he tilted the hand on the tiller and the engine

sputtered and then roared. They cruised south, just outside the reef.

The seafloor shifted from a sandy yellow to green to indigo and then violet. Finally, Héctor cut the engine and the boat bobbed and slowed. They drifted, and Jim looked down through the water to the bright coral that glowed below the surface. Héctor took off his shirt, put on an ancient-looking dive mask, and disappeared over the edge.

As Héctor free-dived, Jim gazed toward the shore. The tip of the old Mayan tower, its limestone blocks glowing white in the sun, was just barely visible to the north.

When Héctor resurfaced, he held a huge conch in each hand, his dive knife clenched between his teeth. He climbed deftly back into the skiff and gave each massive shell a whack, breaking a hole in the suture. With a swift flick of his blade, he killed the creature inside, and after a moment, it slid down through the pink interior and onto his outstretched hand.

On a smooth piece of wood, Héctor expertly chopped the two alien-looking mollusks and dropped them into a dented bowl at his feet. Next, he cut up an onion, three chili peppers, and a tomato and tossed them into the bowl. Finally, he squeezed the juice of two limes over the mixture and gave it a stir. He covered the bowl, put it into a burlap bag, and stowed it in a gunwale.

They fished. Jim reeled in a nice dorado. Héctor caught two mullet and a pompano that he cleaned and threw onto the ice in the cooler with Jim's fish and the beer.

Then he retrieved the bowl of ceviche from the gunwale, and they ate it along with some bread Héctor dug out of his burlap bag. The salsa was sharp and the conch was as delicious as anything Jim had ever tasted. Héctor let the skiff drift as they lay back and drank another beer.

That afternoon, before Jim's shift in the Bar Balché was to begin, Héctor called him to the kitchen. Maria Itzél had grilled Jim's dorado in palm leaves, and the men of the evening crew were gathered around the table waiting to eat.

When Jim arrived, they cheered for him. He had provided for the family meal. To these men, that meant something.

As the months passed, Jim learned the business of Las Posadas as completely as he could. The level of luxury was difficult to exaggerate. While the overall tone was one of rustic simplicity, behind that illusion grinded all the precision and fussiness of a five-star Parisian hotel. No single detail could be overlooked.

Guests were greeted in a luscious forecourt and whisked into an open reception area with a thatched roof, created to resemble the interior of a typical Mayan home but many times larger and, of course, more luxurious. From there, a short, covered walkway led to the Bar Balché, constructed with the same Mayan inspiration but with walls made of heavy wooden shutters that could be opened or closed as called for by the summer rains but were usually wide open. The side opened onto a small paved courtyard and was surrounded by a low wall. Here there were tables shaded by large and brightly colored umbrellas.

From the courtyard, guests had two paths to choose from. Down one, they could sate their hunger at the restaurant, cleverly configured to resemble a number of Mayan-style homes linked together, all with the same soaring rooflines as the reception area and the bar. The walls, made of mud and wattle, were bare and whitewashed. The furniture was comfortable leather stretched over bent cane.

The second path led to the swimming pool, a large rectangular gem surrounded by lounge chairs with plush cushions that matched the vivid hues of the umbrellas in the courtyard.

The pool deck was paved in the same polished limestone from which the ruins, visible in the distance, were constructed, the beige and white relaxing and peaceful. At the distant end of the swimming pool deck, steps led to a corduroy path that wound through low dunes and sea grape to the white Caribbean beach, which stretched invitingly in either direction.

At a subtle distance from the main complex began the accommodations, a string of seventeen individual guest houses on raised pilings that afforded the casitas uninterrupted views of the beach and the sea. From the outside, they resembled the reception building and bar, palapas with pitched roofs of thatched palm. The casitas all had different layouts, with varying numbers of bedrooms, but each featured a sitting room with sea views and a dining room for guests for whom privacy was at a premium.

While guests enjoyed unobstructed views of the beach and ocean from almost everywhere at

the resort, one sight they never had to see was
the resort service building, which was tucked
behind a vast garden near the reception area.
The guests of Las Posadas never lacked for attention, even though they rarely bothered to
pay any to those from whom they received it.

The accoutrements were all first tier: French
bed linens and Turkish towels. The down in
the pillows had been humanely produced in
Cornwall. The sisal of the floor covering was re-
gionally sourced in the Yucatan, but the weaving had been done by the most exclusive English
manufacturers. While the textiles showed in-
flections of local design, they were manufactured by Italian houses that otherwise catered
to haute couture. The furniture? Handmade in
the local style by a Finnish boutique that hired
only the most experienced craftsmen and used
only the finest materials. Philippe Starck created the flatware. Unique works of fine modern
art were handpicked by an agent in Basel. The

bathrooms were Japanese. The spas came from a Belgian firm famous for its copper work.

The food and drink were no different. Grupo Klopp offered its guests exclusive selections. Pol Roger was the house champagne. Penfolds labeled a portion of its Grange line especially for Las Posadas de Altún and the sommelier often pointed the curious in the direction of three Graves and two Saint-Estèphe that were rather more difficult to find.

The caviar was Iranian. The oysters came from a single shoal off Point Judith in Long Island Sound. The foie gras was sourced in the Hudson Valley, though the truffles came from Lombardy. The beef was raised by Mennonite ranchers in Costa Rica without hormones, pesticides, or mechanization. The seafood was caught by dedicated trawlers operating far enough south and east of the resort to experience pristine waters. The coffee was roasted on site. A dairy twenty minutes away produced milk and cream. Only the fruit was truly local, grown on a reserve harvested by Las Posadas staff.

At breakfast, residents made their lunch requests. At lunch, they ordered their evening meals. Nothing came scripted, though the chef always had a suggestion ready. Some mischievous guests tried stumping the kitchen. Only rarely did they succeed.

If guests preferred to have breakfast in bed rather than come to the restaurant, they could request a basket be delivered to their casita every morning at a scheduled time. It held a pot of *café de olla*, a spellbinding blend of coffee and spices and other secrets, along with a fat ceramic bowl full of *huaya*, *zaramullo*, and *guanabana* fruits, peeled that dawn. A palm basket featured an assortment of *pan dulce*, all baked only an hour before. A crystal decanter was filled with a mixture of fresh juice known for sending couples back to bed after only one sip.

And just who were these pampered guests?

To begin, Las Posadas was always fully booked. These were the most elite travelers, people who would never bother inquiring about the cost and never utter any complaint over the final tally. Once a reservation was set, researchers at the Grupo Klopp regional offices in Mérida began assembling a dossier on the booked guest that continued to be filled over time, noting all the intricacies of the guest's stay and any other details about their lifestyle and preferences that could be discovered. Did the guest love pencils? Then pencils there would be: imported Japanese pencils selected from a firm in Osaka that had been making pencils since a wayward German cedarwood and graphite merchant beached there in the 1870s. Las Posadas de Altún went to every end to ensure the success of every visit. For that reason, most of its guests returned, often regularly.

In other words, it was all a long way from Gary, Indiana. Even after six months of living

at the station house in Altún and working nearly every day at Las Posadas, Jim often found
himself waking in disbelief. What was this new
world he had stumbled into?

One morning, Héctor arrived through the back
gate of the compound, having come from the
path from Las Posadas. He circled the station
house and climbed the front steps, where he
found Jim on the porch having his breakfast.

"You ready to go, boss?" Héctor asked.

Jim still didn't know how to take being called
"boss." After feeling forsaken for so long, to be
given a title that implied leadership and control was confusing. He drank what was left in
his coffee bowl and stood.

"What are we up to again?" Jim asked.

"I told you," Héctor said, even though
he hadn't. "It's time. Time for you to meet
Yax Pakal."

They climbed into the white Toyota parked in the yard between the station house and the outbuildings. The vehicle came from the fleet of identical-looking SUVs owned by the resort, and Jim had been told he could use it at his convenience.

Héctor drove. From the compound, a single-lane gravel road led west a short distance to a five-point crossroads. A right turn would take them past the ruins and up to the resort. Left led into the village, where the single track dead-ended at the coral wall at its far end. Acute to that, an even smaller road led to the chapel of San Torcuato, a parish church associated with the saint most highly revered in those parts. Finally, directly west, an unpaved road stretched away from Altún and into the chaos of the jungle. It led twenty straight kilometers before ending at the main coastal road, itself only two lanes wide, but paved at least.

That was the road Héctor took. He accelerated,

seemingly unconcerned with either the condition of the track or what might lie ahead in the
gloom of the jungle.

As they drove, Héctor filled Jim in on the big
boss. Yax Pakal, the *batab* of the southern half
of the state of Quintana Roo, was a rascal. At
least that was what the Mexicans and Europeans
thought of him. But he was Yucatecan, a
real Maya in many respects. He could be as
gentle as a morning fog or as menacing as a
late-afternoon squall. When threatened, or
disobeyed, the dark side of him sprang forth
like the cry of an animal caught in the mouth
of a jaguar. He knew the old ways. All of them.
He had a history.

For the benefit of the Europeans, most often
Yax Pakal played the charming rogue. He soft-
soaped his people's rituals. He was a "good and
observant Christian." And probably he was,
like all his people, who were Catholics and se-
riously devout. Yet, he was still a *batab* and a

priest of Choc Mul. As such, he was the chieftain and magistrate over all things spiritual and temporal for his people, much more than any priest or monsignor might be. The church in Mérida did not even bother sending pastorals to Yax Pakal's lands anymore. While he might smile broadly for the camera of the rare tourist, he had a string of human skulls to wear on the most sacred occasions. More than once, Yax Pakal had held a beating, human heart in his cupped hands.

The people Yax Pakal ruled were a beautiful race, short of stature with large foreheads and patrician noses. They stuck close to their ancient ways. Twice a year they made a sacrifice to Kukulkan, the plumed serpent. Yax Pakal led the rituals, which always involved blood.

"Listen," Héctor said to close out the lesson, "Yax Pakal, he's a different hombre. Different from us. He's from the old way. In the end, he's a good guy. But you want to be respectful of him. There's freaky things that go on. This isn't our world. This is the jungle, amigo. This is the old world of the *people*. And once you go inside it, you are their guest. You don't have any rights or privileges. You just do what they say."

A sense of danger descended over Jim. With each turn, the road became less perceptible. The jungle began slapping at the windshield. Vines poked in the windows. The path was mottled with distant light, like swimming deep in the ocean. Up there, somewhere, there was sky. But a lot of dense foliage and wild animals and who knew what else was in between.

With time, the jungle began to withdraw, and they entered cultivated land. Jim couldn't tell what was growing, only that the fields were orderly and well maintained. Soon Héctor turned into a sort of corral, which surrounded a scattering of typical native structures, stone oval walls with steeply peaked thatched roofs.

Jim climbed from the Toyota and slowly

turned to scout the scene. The place looked deserted, except for a flock of chickens pecking in the yard.

Then four men emerged from the largest structure. They were large men, dressed indifferently in Western clothes, but with a military bearing about them.

"They want you inside," Héctor said. "Remember—we're guests."

Jim entered through the low doorway. Inside was a small, painted wooden table. A man sat in a straight-back chair beside it, and across the table was an identical chair, only empty. The man stared at Jim, who paused on the threshold for what felt like an eternity. He pulled a red bandanna from his pocket and mopped his forehead, damp from the jungle's humidity and his nerves.

There was something about that motion that stirred the powerful-looking man sitting in the stiff chair.

"You," he said. "That bandanna, that cloth you carry. Bring it to me."

Jim walked forward, holding out the bandanna.

The man took the cloth, examined it, and returned it to Jim.

"You must excuse me," the seated man said. He spoke English clearly and without any accent. "But my men have an antipathy to strangers. Particularly European strangers. You see, their parents and grandparents suffered." He shook his head dolefully, as if the Spanish Conquest was a fresh and painful memory.

He gestured graciously for Jim to be seated. At one end of the otherwise empty room, a fire burned in the ground behind a stone screen.

The men withdrew to the edges of the room, one at the center of each wall.

"First, before we begin, I am Yax Pakal," he said with an exaggerated courtesy. "I must ask you. Who are you?"

Jim felt as if he were in a dream and playing a role he had not auditioned for. Acting on instinct, he removed the ring from his right hand and set it on the painted table. Jim had done a little research and learned that it was a jaguar head carved into the jade stone and that the jaguar represented the Hero Twins, the ball-playing brothers from the sacred Maya text the Popol Vuh, who had descended to the underworld and outwitted the gods of Hell. On their return to Earth, they carried with them the secret for ascending to the world that was to come. The twins were sometimes depicted as the spirit and animal forms of the jaguar.

Yax Pakal studied the ring closely, but only for a moment. Then he flashed Jim a shiny smile, his remarkably white teeth edged in gold, and put his own hand, palm down, on the table next to Jim's ring.

An exact duplicate, its oval jade intaglio

featuring the head of a jaguar, encircled Yax Pakal's dark, chubby finger.

"Don Carlos," Yax Pakal said, "he and I, back in the days, the early times, we had plenty of adventures. He was my friend. Tell me, how is Don Carlos today?"

Jim wasn't sure how to respond. There felt something diminishing in telling this Maya chieftain that his old comrade in arms was a social studies teacher at a high school in the Midwest.

"He always talks too much!" Yax Pakal continued, giving Jim a brief stay. "On and on with his Kant this and Kierkegaard that! I bet those pupils rue the day they drew Don Carlos for a teacher!" He laughed heartily.

As if his laughter were an agreed-upon cue, women entered the hut carrying wooden bowls of steaming food. Jim's gaze followed them only briefly, then he replied truthfully. "He's very popular, actually. The students love him. They are remarkably loyal to him."

The mood in the smoky hut, with its dirt floor and grass roof, changed utterly and instantly.

Yax Pakal leaned forward, his dark eyes serious and possibly violent. "There is no man more loyal to Don Carlos than me," he said. "They do not know what loyalty means, *mi amigo*. Loyalty is to die for a man."

"He saved my life," Jim said, suddenly overwhelmed with emotion, the words tumbling out as he fingered the precious ring on the table. He had not thought it through completely before, but, yes, Chuck Marlow had saved his life.

"And that," said Yax Pakal, placing his hand over Jim's, "is why you and I, amigo, are compadres. And we shall always be."

Yax Pakal broke into a wide and compelling smile, and with it the tension in the room broke as well. Jim felt the men at the edges of the hut relax, and a weight lifted from his chest. He smiled, too.

"Eat, hombres! Eat!" Yax Pakal urged, and the men swarmed to the line of women, grabbing plates and piling them high with tamales, poc chuc, and squash.

With a full stomach, Jim felt emboldened to ask the *batab* a question. "Is it true what they say? That you once tore out the beating heart from an enemy and ate it?"

Yax Pakal only smiled. "When you're young and full of life," he said, "you do some pretty crazy things."

Héctor and his wife, Valeria, had been blessed with a late surprise after having raised five girls in Altún. They had a handsome eleven-year-old boy named Sammy whom they both adored. Rare was the time when Sammy was not either helping his mother or working alongside his father at Las Posadas. He was something of a shared child there; everyone loved Sammy.

And it was Sammy who came to the station house with a mischievous grin one afternoon an hour or so before Jim's shift was set to begin.

"Don Jaime," he said, "there's something for you to see." He beckoned with his hands, ushering Jim to come with him.

"*Qué pasó, amigo?*" Jim said, trying out the Spanish he'd starting picking up from conversation with Héctor and other resort staff.

"Just somebody Papa said you'd want to meet."

Jim and Sammy walked out the back gate, across the ruins, and to Las Posadas. Once beneath the thatched roof of the reception area, Sammy threw his head in the direction of Bar Balché, then ran off, banging through the doors to the kitchen down the hallway.

Jim walked into the bar. And there she was. He recognized her shape from behind. She wore the same red kerchief in her dark hair, along with a backless red smock, a short jean skirt, and a pair of well-broken-in, dark-brown cowboy boots. Her bare legs, from the hem of the skirt until they disappeared into the neck of the boots, appeared even more exposed, somehow, stretching between denim and leather. She sat at the bar chatting with a guest.

Malinda's ghost was alive and well and right in front of him. From nowhere, he began to hear the hacking of chopper blades. He shuddered involuntarily. A wave of nausea rose and crested in his throat.

Crash and splash.

He felt himself tumble through a false awakening. A dream within a dream. An REM continuum.

The woman was tall like Malinda. Slim like Malinda. Dark like Malinda, with sunglasses perched atop her head. Like Malinda.

From a distance, Jim watched as she got up from her perch and walked around the bar, where he finally got a look at her features. He was both relieved and disappointed to find a beautiful yet unfamiliar face framed by the dark hair and sunglasses. His nerves immediately began to settle, and he bemusedly watched the mystery woman shake a drink with a theatrical flourish and pour out two glasses, one for herself and one for the man she chatted with.

They talked a bit more, then the guest finished his drink, kissed her on the cheek, and disappeared toward the beach.

Jim waited a moment, wondering if she'd notice him where he was, then decided to come closer and introduce himself.

"So," she said, not looking up from her phone but noting Jim's approach, "you're New Guy."

"I am," Jim said. "As of about six months ago. I'm Jim."

"Uh-huh." Her eyes darted to a trio of guests who entered the bar from the direction of the casitas.

"Hello!" they called in unison, in plummy British accents. The woman in the denim skirt leaped up and they pulled her into a group hug. The man of the trio held out a bottle of very expensive champagne, and a broad smile crossed her face. One of the women carried four flutes, two in each hand. The man gestured with the bottle, and Jim's mysterious new acquaintance—if he could call her that, given he hadn't actually gotten her name—shot a quick farewell glance at Jim before following her friends down the path to the beach.

Much later that night, after he had closed Bar Balché and returned to the station house, Jim relaxed in a chair tipped back against a wall of the wood-planked veranda.

A figure stepped onto the porch. In the darkness, Jim could just make out the red hue of her top.

"Jewel," she said.

Jim recognized the name instantly. "O'Connor's daughter?" he asked, his tone a mixture of surprise and sudden comprehension.

"Supposedly."

He chuckled awkwardly. "You're not sure?"

"I don't have a strong recollection of them screwing, if that's what you mean."

Jim laughed again. "I guess," he said.

"Neither does Cornelius, I suspect," she added, "if you catch my drift."

Jim regarded her in silence. "You live here?" he asked.

"You mean at the station house? I do," she said. "I mean, I have. I've been away for a while."

"Like, years?"

"Like, since the first night you were here."

Right. Jim flashed back to his ethereal vision of the woman with the red kerchief. Malinda's ghost. Now here in the flesh.

"Then where have you been?" he asked.

"I had some business to attend to." She took the other chair from the rustic table and dragged it across the rough planks of the floor until it was opposite Jim. She sank into it, her back to the fancifully painted wooden railing. "Up north."

"Up north?"

"In that direction, yes."

Jim couldn't decipher her expression, but it was clear he wasn't going to get a more definitive answer, for whatever reason.

"But now you're back."

"For a bit," she said.

"Do you have a . . . a position?" Jim fumbled his words. "I mean, are you employed, or I guess, I mean, you know, down here—"

"I work . . ." Her voice trailed off. "For Antonio and Héctor. Just like you, big boy."

"Well, I don't really have a job, per se. It's more of a position?" Jim's voice rose in his own puzzlement.

"*Yo tambien*," Jewel said. "A *position*."

Jim didn't know whether to be offended, intimidated, or attracted. So, he was all three.

"This is a crazy place, Jim," she said. "It's an adult dose of everything. Where do you come from? Hoochie-cooch or someplace? The back-end of brackish America?"

"Gary, Indiana, actually," Jim said.

"Like I said. Hoochie Cooch Junction. Gary, Indiana. *My lord*."

"It gets a bad rap, but it's not what people say it is."

"Really, Jim? Is that your final answer?"

Now he really didn't know how to feel.

"I guess," he said.

"You're cute, Jim," she said. "I think I'll keep you."

And she stood, leaving the chair empty by the railing, and stomped in her brown cowboy boots into the station house.

***

The next morning at Las Posadas, Héctor and Jim attended the staff meeting in the service building. They were joined by top chef Maria Itzél, the resort's accountant, the young woman who managed reservations, the chief housekeeper, and the head of grounds, who kept the resort looking like some billionaire's personal botanical garden. Antonio led the meeting, as always, and started with a run through the numbers, the supplies, the orders, and a few guest peculiarities to anticipate. After a quick report from chef, reservations, and grounds, he adjourned the meeting. But he asked if Héctor and Jim might stay behind for a quick word.

"I got another threat," Antonio said. "It's the cartel. Los Siguientes. They think they can muscle us for protection money. Monterrey says no go, of course. But Monterrey is a long way away. We won't do it, obviously, but we need to keep our eyes out. Be on the lookout for funny business. Sabotage. I don't know how we handle it if it escalates. These guys, they're new in town. *Norteños*. Bad men all around."

Afterward, Héctor filled Jim in.

The Guadalajara-based Siguientes had first spread north to Juarez and Nuevo Laredo on the US border, then had begun expanding south and east, through Vera Cruz and Tabasco and finally into the Yucatan. Now it controlled the drug trade in the north of the peninsula, from Mérida to Cancún, and down the east coast through the highly profitable Maya Riviera. The horror stories that had once been limited to Ciudad Juárez and Nuevo Laredo had started getting reported from the Hotel District in Cancún.

And the cartel wasn't finished. It wanted the whole peninsula. But it had failed to seize the territory farther south. It had yet to defeat Yax Pakal.

Los Siguientes were *norteños*, men of mixed Spanish and native ancestry, descendants of the conquistadors and the famously savage Cáhita warriors. Their background and beliefs were utterly different from those of the Maya of the jungle lowlands. They might as well have been from different continents, which, arguably, they were.

Under Yax Pakal, the people of the Balam, as the ancestral area was known, had developed a thriving suite of cash-producing products. Specifically, they made and moved many of the psychoactive materials that had gained such prestige in the new millennium: balché, sativa, and the potently hallucinogenic okox buttons and toad skins. Each was a small business, and together they formed the lifeblood of hard currency with which Yax Pakal kept his people solvent. For every rich white kid on his "journey" there was a Maya kid, or maybe even a family, just getting by. They sold to the highest bidder.

The demand was always greater than the ability to produce.

Now Los Siguientes wanted to control that.

The barefoot girls who tended the crops, the old ladies who prepared the product, and the men who delivered it to the various drops—all of them, and all their families, depended on the security of their network. Were they to lose the groves of lilac trees whose bark was boiled, or the location of a trusted and recurring bed of the sacred mushrooms, or a holy cenote whose caverns hid the cane toads whose skins were fat with magic, tragedy would ensue. The delicate jungle web on which all Yax Pakal's people depended would be shredded.

And now the rumor was that Los Siguientes were coming and coming stronger than they ever had before.

They were invading.

9

The next day was a Wednesday, Jim's single day off. In the late afternoon, Jewel knocked on the door of his room.

"Want to see something interesting?" she asked. "Want to see what this place is really all about?"

"I thought Las Posadas was what it was all about," Jim said.

"The other half," she said. "The heavy part."

"Sure," Jim said, climbing from his hammock and stepping into his huaraches with their tire-tread soles.

He followed Jewel across the hot and dusty station yard and out the rusted iron gate. She traversed the narrow lane to the five-point crossroads and chose the path that led to the Chapel of San Torcuato.

The older locals, the ones who only spoke the language of the village, revered its patron saint. They believed San Torcuato communicated directly with the greatest powers of the pantheon of the old ways. San Torcuato was the people's champion. He was the one who would lead the way when the time of destruction came, who would show the people of the Balam how to step from this world into the next.

As Jim and Jewel approached the limestone threshold, she paused and took a folded red silk scarf from the back pocket of her jeans. She unfurled it, folded it once diagonally, and tied it over her dark hair. Then she turned to Jim.

"The Festival of San Torcuato next month is the biggest event of the year," Jewel said. "It begins with a procession, prayers, and a feast, and after the initial rituals are complete, it transforms into three fabulous days of parades and fairs and feasting. Which of course includes an element of drunkenness. On the highest holy days everyone, children included, drink *p'os*."

"*P'os?*"

"Oh, boy. Of course, you don't know *p'os*. This is your first feast day. It starts out as balché—yes, like the name of the resort bar," she added when she saw the glimmer of recognition in his eyes, "which is fermented lilac tree bark and honey. To make *p'os,* other stuff goes in. 'Secret' stuff, naturally. It sits a year in these big stone vats. And it comes out with a kick like an otter's pocket."

"'A kick like an otter's pocket'?" Jim laughed at the unusual expression.

"You'll find out," she said with a playful smirk.

In addition to the revelry, she went on to explain, the villagers offered San Torcuato prayer and sacred gifts. They would prostrate themselves before him to pray for benevolence in the stormy season to come. Because San Torcuato was also Huracan, the god of wind and rain. The god of destruction. One day, it was written, San Torcuato would announce the arrival of the Lord of the Eleventh Katun, who would come from the sea from the east, and the great flood that would erase this world and usher in the next.

Jim looked out to the ocean, which was low and green and calm in the distance. Then his eyes flicked inland to the jungle, which shot up in a dense wall of foliage almost a hundred feet high. Between were the chapel and the small fields that the villagers kept heroically free of encroachment.

"*Do not show us your wrath, holy saint,*" Jewel recited. "*Spare us the scourge of your anger. We acknowledge our sins. We offer our penance.*"

The birds and monkeys tittered loudly with

crepuscular chatter, as though they were offering penance of their own.

Jim gave Jewel a funny look, and she smiled. "Come," she said and gestured him to follow as she finally entered the church.

The small chapel was identical in most ways to a thousand others that were spread across the Maya lowlands and into Chiapas and Guatemala. The finest work was in the mahogany door, hung on heavy iron hinges. Inside, the floor was simple terracotta tile swept clean with old fan-shaped brooms. There was no furniture.

The altar was draped in white cloth and crowded with as many statues of saints as it could hold. Most of the figures—including multiple Josephs and Marys, as well as numerous other duplicate forms, due to the sheer volume—represented not their namesakes, but various Maya gods. Each was outfitted in a native costume and wore a small mirror hanging from a ribbon around its neck.

The air smelled of burning copal. The only light came from two high windows and from candles in glass jars illuminating the chapel's periphery.

A huge wooden cross, wrapped entirely in purple cloth, was propped against one nave wall and stretched from the floor to nearly the ceiling. At its base, an old woman in a white blouse, an embroidered skirt, and a richly decorated red shawl sat cross-legged on the stone. On one side of her, incense wafted from a thick stone bowl, and on the other sat a clay pitcher and two clay cups. A younger woman crouched in front of her, and they spoke in whispers. A group of villagers waited in a casual line.

"This is Doña Lora, the village healer," Jewel said, also in a whisper. "She is a shaman, a medicine woman. She directs the people to the ways to solve their problems."

"Problems?" Jim asked. "Like illness? Sickness?"

"Problems," Jewel repeated. "These people, they do not differentiate so much. They do not distinguish between problems of the people and problems of the head and problems of the chest. Anyway, she cures them all."

The shaman poured from the clay pitcher into the two cups and handed one to the other woman, then touched her own cup to the woman's shoulder before they both drank.

"What are they drinking?"

"This is the healing drink," Jewel said. "Used for sickness. It's the balché I was telling you about. At least it is to start. Each healer adds her own secrets to the mixture."

"What about that?" Jim asked, nodding toward the giant purple cross. "What's the story there?"

"That's the Talking Cross," Jewel said. "It is very important to the people. It's the cross that leads them. The prophecy teaches that San Torcuato will signal the beginning of the end of the world."

"Right," Jim said, trying to remember her words from earlier. "The Lord of the something or other, coming from the sea?"

Jewel groaned comically. "The Lord *of the Eleventh Katun,* coming from the sea *from the east,* Jim. Those details are very important."

Jim wondered why but didn't ask. He had arrived from the east himself, out of the morning sun. Coming from the east didn't feel very sacred then, and it certainly hadn't been sacred when the Spanish arrived hundreds of years ago. He failed to see why it would matter so much with the prophecy, but then, he failed to buy in to prophecies in the first place.

The young woman rose from her spot in front of Doña Lora, genuflected, and left the chapel. The next villager in line quickly replaced her, and the pair began talking in hushed tones.

When Jim and Jewel finished looking around, a clear night had set. The swiftness of dusk at this latitude always surprised Jim. Mars burned brightly above.

They walked back along the track toward the station house in silence.

Jim and Jewel began to spend much of their time together. They rose with the sun in the mornings and drank coffee and ate fried plantains. Their conversation came easily and picked up always where it had left off. Jim learned that Jewel, for all her casual flippancy, had a remarkable intelligence. She was sophisticated in ways that Jim, in his Midwestern earnestness, could not match.

Her character was a sort of puzzle. She felt as comfortable with the people of the village and jungle as she did with the wealthy and sophisticated foreigners she encountered at the resort.

She knew the local history, both the recent and the ancient and mythical. She understood intuitively the ethnography of the place, the world of the Yucatan and of Altún. However, even though she was born there, her mysterious lineage kept her a foreigner in the eyes of the natives, and she saw their lives through the eyes of an outsider. A very observant outsider. She was tough, floating between worlds, and completely aware.

She confirmed what Jim had been told about her childhood and seemed to not know—or really even care—who her parents were. She scoffed at the absurd notion Cornelius could be her father and told Jim her mother had left her nothing other than a well-worn rosary in black onyx and a folded slip of blue paper containing the name Rosemary Page and a phone number.

Rosemary had come to visit when Jewel was one year old, and from then on she'd dropped in several times a year, always making sure

Jewel was well cared for and had everything she needed. When Jewel asked about her parents, Rosemary would hold her tight and tell her that when she was older, she would know more. Eventually Jewel had stopped asking. Now that Jewel was an adult, Rosemary only came occasionally, but they still exchanged letters, and Jewel thought of her as a fairy godmother of sorts.

While Jewel had recognizable aspects of Maya physiognomy, she was also quite tall and slim, with dark, full hair that danced in the breeze rather than running dead straight down her back. She had an almost miraculous strength, as if she exercised like a prison inmate, which she did not. Jim never saw her do any more than walk around the resort and the village and engage in the same sorts of chores anyone else might take on. Yet she was naturally sinuous, rangy, and powerful, and had been since she was a child.

For the Maya women of Altún who had raised her, she was a fifth child, a favorite niece, and a bit of a headache as she was headstrong and independent. She had been a monkey, a tomboy, a girl who got up to all the same trouble as the boys in the village. She had little interest in the things that occupied the other girls her age.

To the staff of Las Posadas, she was a lovable scamp, always underfoot. As she grew older, it was understood by direction of each successive manager of the resort, sent to Altún from the company headquarters, that she was to be protected, encouraged, and, whenever possible, nurtured. She grew into a beautiful woman who was the daughter of the station and Las Posadas while at the same time nobody's child at all.

Jim locked like a jigsaw puzzle piece into her mystery. In stark opposition, in nearly perfect complement, his history was anything but a mystery. Indeed, it was all too well-known. He knew from exactly where he came. He knew where and when and how his life turned on a dime, the exact moment, captured by a lucky photographer's telephoto lens, that made it so he could never return, and sent him on this journey that led to Altún, to Las Posadas. To Jewel.

Jewel and Jim continued to visit the Chapel of San Torcuato every chance they got. The women there began to greet them. Even Doña Lora, while not welcoming, exactly, began to acknowledge their existence.

Jim began identifying things needing fixing with the chapel and its grounds. It was, after all, a structure with shallow foundations that had stood in that spot for nearly five hundred years. The roof of the southern transept had begun to leak, so with the help of workmen borrowed from Las Posadas, Jim had it patched. A wall had begun to erode after a season of unusually heavy rain. First, Jim organized the village men to engage in the long, hot work of digging, and sometimes drilling, a proper drainage system into the lime substrate. Next, after repointing the sagging wall, made originally from stones that had been hauled from the Maya ruins on the other side of the village, Jim oversaw the re-mudding of the whole wall, a task that took five days and the help of almost the entire village.

The repairs continued inside, where two timber braces had sagged and needed support. Again, Jim turned to the maintenance crew of Las Posadas, and he was pleased to find that Antonio never raised an eyebrow at the use of men and materials. The villagers, likewise, pitched in with alacrity. No one needed to be asked twice to lend their time to repair the Chapel of San Torcuato.

Throughout it all, Jim rose mightily in the eyes of the people of Altún. There had never been tensions between the villagers and Las

Posadas, as the Klopps had always been very
generous to the people of Altún. But the resort was an entirely different world from the
village, even for the villagers who worked there.
It was removed from the ancient rhythms and
cadences of the village. No one from the resort
had ever broken through that barrier and reso-
nated with the locals.

Jim changed that. Maybe it was being an
Indiana kid. Maybe it was the companionship
of the mysterious Jewel. Maybe it was something else. Whatever it was, the villagers began
to respect and slightly revere Jim. He wasn't just
a gringo. He was a *batab*.

Batab. Chieftain, ruler, priest—none of
those quite fully captured the meaning. "Lord"
came close.

Among the villagers, the date of Jim's arrival
to Altún began to assume a providential aura.
Certainly, there was no easy parsing of the local
traditions. Before the Conquista, the village of

Altún had already been separated from the better parts of late Maya civilization: the lowlands to the north and the highlands to the southwest. Their ways had become divergent from those of the better-known city-states, themselves under times of great stress and change. The people of Altún persisted in their pagan ways for a long time after the arrival of the Spaniards, if only because it took a hundred years more after Cortés's arrival for any Christians at all to reach the most remote parts of the southern peninsula.

As with most places in the New World, the villagers of Altún took a buffet approach to the religion brought unto them by the Spanish. And while they held faithfully to the promise of a second coming by the Lord and Savior, Jesus Christ, at the same time, the people of Altún held other beliefs equally firmly.

Huracán was the god of the sky and destruction from above.

The River Shark god would bring destruction from the fresh waters.

And San Torcuato, when his time came, would announce the beginning of the end of time with an announcement of the arrival of the Lord of the Eleventh Katun. This mystical appearance would signal the end of this world and usher in the commencement of the next.

The Lord of the Eleventh Katun was prophesized to arrive by sea, from the east. His eyes would be blue in color.

He would come at a time of great turmoil. He would come at a time of fire and blood.

Jim heard the rumors. He didn't go in for them, or believe he was the Katun. But he also had come to realize how much he didn't know. He didn't know a lot. This was a strange place and a mystical one. He wasn't about to disabuse anybody on any subject he did not understand himself.

The river shark is a totem of fire,
he is a totem of blood.
He devours the children;
he devours the wives. Dying children,
dying wives. He is rich.
He ends time.

10

Bar Balché was hopping. Jim had already served the older couples—men tidily dressed in blazers and slacks ordering brandy or good bourbon, neat, while their spouses in pearls and floral sheaths invariably requested a white wine to nurse. Occasionally a more adventuresome lady would try one of Jim's champagne concoctions: fizz mixed with the renowned juice of the breakfast basket and a drop of pomegranate liqueur.

Now he was busy with the thirtysomething set, who tended to travel in groups of couples. He was pouring for a group of pretty people from Los Angeles who had flown down on two Gulfstream jets. Owned, not rented.

Jim recognized one of the men from earlier in the day. When they'd first met, the man had posed with an arrogant air until Jim failed to look impressed. Then he'd introduced himself—Nick Dimitriou, the *actor*—and Jim had feigned recognition, figuring he must be D-list at best. His wealth clearly hadn't come from his acting career.

Jim had mixed Nick one of his specialty Bloody Marys, based on a recipe K-Tell had taught him in Iraq. The spice was the key, and one of K-Tell's girlfriends back at Pax River in Maryland sent a special blend in care packages along with the main ingredient, contraband vodka disguised as designer bottled water. Jim had created a similar spice mixture at Las Posadas with local flavors, and Nick had liked the drink so much he'd asked for a second. And then a third.

"Hey, babe," Nick said now to the tanned blonde who trailed somewhat indifferently after him as he approached the bar. "Here's the guy I told you about. The one who made me that knockout Bloody."

The woman, wearing a billowy white Mexican dress with orange stitching at the neck, gazed at Jim with bored eyes. Then with a suggestive tilt of her shoulders, she revealed that she wore nothing else beneath her dress.

Nick frowned at her gesture and pulled her to his side. "Come on, let's try one," he said.

"I don't want a damn Bloody Mary at nine o'clock at night," she snapped.

"Right," Nick said, releasing his grip around her shoulder. "Good point. I think I'll have a"—he slapped his hands together and looked upward, as if there would be a fast-food menu over Jim's head—"margarita. That's it! A margarita. Babe?"

"Beer," she said. "That beer I like."

Nick looked stymied, as though he'd never seen her drink a beer before.

"Montejo?" Jim suggested as he grabbed a pair of limes for the margarita. Montejo was the house beer, made in Mérida.

The woman shrugged. Her dress could cover one shoulder or the other, but not, it seemed, both.

"Damn good," Nick said, after taking a sip from the salt-rimmed glass Jim set in front of him. "Not as good as the Bloody, but probably the best margarita I ever had, too. This place," he said, turning again to his companion, "it's like, everything I have here is the best version of it I ever did."

"Tell me about it," she said, rolling her eyes and taking a swig from her bottle of beer.

Nick, still marveling over his margarita, held up the glass and walked across the room to where his party was settling just outside the eaves of the thatched roof. The blonde lingered.

"You live down here or is it an exchange thing or indentured servitude or slavery or what?" she asked Jim, crawling onto one of the leather-strap stools.

"Slavery," Jim said. "Pirates traded me for an old transistor radio."

"They wanted to listen to baseball, probably," the woman said and downed her Montejo. She plunked the bottle onto the bar.

"Another?" Jim asked.

The woman put her hands on the rail and leaned in, as if deciding. "Okay," she said, after giving Jim ample time to glance down her dress. "Let's do a shot."

Jim set out a tequila glass and reached for the *añejo*, aged, exclusive, and exotic. He poured her out a shot.

"No, no, no, no, no," she said. "You, too."

Jim scratched his chin. The etiquette was to take one when offered, within reason. Without looking, he could tell that Nick, now standing with the rest of his party, was watching them. He went ahead and poured a second shot.

"C'mon," she said.

They both raised their glasses. Jim let her go first. Rather than throwing it back, she sipped it. She clearly knew her tequila. Jim followed suit, gratefully. It was too good a tequila to down in a gulp.

"Pirate booty," she said.

"You could say that," Jim said.

"You look familiar to me."

Jim couldn't tell if she was drunk and flirting or really did recognize him.

"Guess my birthday," she said.

"April eighteenth," Jim said quickly, the date having popped randomly into his mind.

She looked mildly stricken, as if Jim had thrown her off her game.

"Andy!" she yelled across the room. The bar went quiet. "What's my birthday?"

"It's not today, Heather, sorry."

"Nick!"

"April eighteenth," he said. "Wednesday's child is full of woe!" The group sitting at the tables around him laughed.

"You can walk me back to my casita," she said to Jim.

"You know I can't."

"Eff your mother," Heather said. She finished her tequila and threw the glass to the terracotta floor. She slid off her stool, kicking it over, then ran out of bar.

Nick looked up with the rest of his group, shook his head, and stood. He followed her, shooting Jim a look Jim couldn't quite interpret as he took off down the lit path that led from the deck back toward the casitas.

The rest of the group fell silent, staring like prairie dogs into the darkness. Nick's voice floated back to the bar, low and imploring. Heather shouted an obscenity. Jim could hear her sandals slapping as she ran farther away.

The group finished their drinks and peeled away in couples, until no one was left in Bar Balché but Jim. He relished the quiet.

Jim took his usual shortcut back to the station house via the ruins, passing first one of the pyramids, the steps of which he'd climbed one day with Héctor and Sammy, and then the colonnaded building, which he'd learned had been a ceremonial structure called a nunnery. He skirted the ball court—an interesting I-shape lined with steep walls, two of which had small vertical hoops near the top—and came finally to the tower, the structure for which the site was best known. Its image had once adorned the fifty-peso note, but that was many years before.

As he usually did, he paused for a moment to admire it, glowing in the moonlight on its promontory, the placid black sea in the distance. Suddenly a dark figure shot up from the grass beside him, and Jim instinctively reached to his side for the gun he no longer carried. Just as startled, the bearded figure looked back at Jim and bleated its warning: "Ma-a-a-a." The old billy goat the villagers kept at the ruins to browse the grass then trotted toward the nunnery, leaving Jim shaking his head at his own silliness, his heartbeat slowly returning to a normal cadence.

But the incident had put him on edge, and in the moonlight, the ruins cast long shadows that Jim for the first time found malevolent. How much blood had been spilled on that ground in the centuries Altún had been an active settlement, he wondered. How many children and prisoners had been bled out to a watchful crowd? It came easy to romanticize the place, with its striking architecture and splendid views of the blue-green ocean. But it was also once a place of great violence and death.

He was lost in thought as he entered the

courtyard of the compound and tread lightly toward the station house. He barely had time to register motion in his peripheral vision before something hard slammed into his side and he was tackled to the dirt. A boot connected with his stomach and he doubled over, the air rushing from his lungs like a compressed bellows. Another boot struck his ribs over and over, and yet another lashed out from behind and kicked one of his kidneys. He moaned in agony, lacking the breath to make a louder noise. The pummeling continued for several more moments, then stopped as suddenly as it had begun.

Jim coiled into the tightest ball he could to protect himself from the next onslaught, but it never came. He slowly opened his eyes, which adjusted quickly to the low light from the moon, to find four pairs of boots on the ground in front of him, and then a fifth stepped in front of them. Jim drew his gaze higher, taking in

the hulking form topped with a cowboy hat. It
let out a whooping laugh, then spoke.

"Hey, hombre, what you doing in the dirt
like that? Getting your nice shirt all dirty." He
laughed again. "I got a message for you. From
a friend of yours."

Jim's heart pounded in his ears, but he realized the fact the assault had switched to speech
probably meant they weren't going to hurt him
anymore. "What friend?" he asked, tentatively.

"You got a new friend, amigo. He's going to
be a good friend to you. He's going to take care
of you good."

"I'm not looking for new friends."

"Oh, amigo, I think so. I think you are very
lonely here at your fancy posada."

"I can handle myself."

"Yes, yes, but think about this, amigo. What
if you have a new good friend who take care of
you? Look after you. Make sure nothing *happen* to you. Or to the pretty *chica bonita* you

got back there." The man nodded toward the station house, which had remained dark this entire time, and Jim's heart pounded anew with worry for Jewel.

"You touch her and I'll kill you," Jim growled.

"No, amigo," said the man and laughed his sinister laugh, as the four men behind him leaned forward menacingly. "You no kill nobody. You never kill nobody, do you, hombre? Isn't that why you here? You never kill nobody?"

Thock-thock-thock.

The Black Hawks circled the carnage in the cafeteria, as Jim's mind was spattered with red. Amber Parker tackled Kevin White, much as Jim had been taken down just moments before by these strangers. He pushed the images from his head. That was in the past. He wasn't that Jim Lord anymore.

"What do you want?" he spat.

"See, very simple. Very easy." The man reached into one of the pockets on his western shirt for a pack of cigarettes. He shook one out and lit it. "You get the hell out of here and go back to where you come from. Is that so hard, amigo? Good for your health, too."

"I'm not leaving," Jim said. "It's you who needs to leave. Now. And don't come back."

"Oh, I don't think so, amigo. See, there is a real man, called Sherif Ali, and you've made him mad, hanging around, acting like a boss. He is the new jefe around here. Not you. And not that *pinche* old man who lives in the jungle. Sherif Ali is the one who is going to tell you from now on."

"Maybe you didn't understand me," Jim said. "I'm not afraid of this Sherif Ali or you or your thugs."

"Not afraid, eh?" The man chuckled yet again. "From what I hear, you're afraid a lot. You like to run. But you know what? Maybe you should run again now." He threw his cigarette into the dust, then held his hands apart and shrugged. "You don't have much time to make up your mind."

As he turned, he kicked a puff of dirt into Jim's face, leaving him coughing and blinking the grit out of his eyes as the man disappeared through the gate with his henchmen in tow. They piled into a large black pickup and sped off.

Jim stumbled to his feet, clutching his side. His ribs were sore, but he didn't think any were broken, and he managed a smile, despite everything. El Altún was starting to really feel like home, and he wasn't going to let anyone drive him away.

The next morning, Jewel was already on the veranda sipping her coffee when Jim came out. He moved stiffly as he joined her.

"What happened to you?" she asked, giving him a dubious once-over.

"Oh, I was just kicked around like a soccer ball by four Siguientes, then told by their leader to leave town. No biggie."

Jewel leaned in with saucer eyes. "What?! Where? Last night? How the hell . . ."

Jim filled her in on the events of the previous night, and she gasped at all the appropriate moments. When he was done, she paused, reflecting on what he'd told her.

"Maybe you should think about it," she finally said. "These Siguientes dudes are bad. I've heard the stories. There's an army of these guys, and they'll keep coming. There's only one of you."

"I got that," Jim said, laughing despite himself.

"No one here can protect you," Jewel said. "Not Héctor. Maybe not even Yax Pakal. I don't know why you came to Altún, and I've liked having you around, but this might be the end of the road for you here."

"But I don't want to leave," he insisted. "And why me, anyway? Why now?"

"Don't you see?" she said. "Because you replaced Cornelius. If Cornelius was still the station master, he would have sold out to them. I wouldn't be surprised if he was the one who told them where to find you and when."

"But I'm just a bartender. A gringo. I've been here, what, seven months? I'm a nobody in Altún and a nobody to these cartel thugs."

"That's not what the villagers think. And that's not what Yax Pakal says."

"What does Yax Pakal say?"

"He says you carry the Jaguar ring. That you are here to protect them."

"Who's 'them'?"

"The people. The villagers. Isn't that what you did up in the States? Protect people?"

"That was a long way from here," Jim said softly.

"You know what the villagers have started

calling you, don't you? *Batab* Jim. Lord Jim."
She put her hand atop his and squeezed.

He pulled away abruptly, pushed out his
chair, and stood. "I've got to figure out what
I've gotten myself into. I don't know about being anyone's lord, but I'm not running from a
fight with these thugs. I'm not going anywhere."

Right at that moment, Cornelius O'Connor
stepped onto the veranda, followed as always
by a limping P'en. Jim hadn't seen the duo in
days. He'd almost managed to forget Cornelius
was still around, especially because it seemed
he had no reason to be.

Clad in a clean guayabera and a pair of billow-
ing linen trousers, Cornelius struck a dramatic
pose and patently feigned attitude of alarm.

"Why, Jim, did I just hear you're thinking of
leaving?" he cried. "Why on earth would you
do that?" He dabbed his forehead with a sweat-
stained bandanna. "Did something . . . *happen?*"

His tone said what his words only hinted at:

Jewel was right, Cornelius not only knew about the ambush, he had likely helped set it up. Jim considered playing coy, but his anger got the better of him.

"You, Cornelius!" he barked. "You know exactly what happened!"

Cornelius jumped in place, a tiny hop as though he were avoiding an invisible jump rope. Then he recovered his air of innocence and replied smugly, "Who, me? I have no idea what you're talking about." P'en lurked behind him, his scraggly teeth bared in defense of his boss.

"Take your things, Cornelius," Jim said, his mouth twisted with fury. "I don't trust you in the house anymore. I want you in that shed over there." He pointed toward the cannery. "You're lucky I don't just kick you out, because you have no use here anyway."

Cornelius's round eyes bulged at the implied threat. He drew himself as tall as his squat frame allowed and opened his mouth to argue, but then catching himself and realizing that his position might be more tenuous than he had suspected, he spread his hands and bowed to Jim respectfully.

"Yes, yes, yes," he said. "Of course, señor. As you please."

Cornelius noticed Jewel sitting quietly at the table and collected himself with a desperate attempt at poise.

"You heard the señor," he barked at Jewel. "Go! Collect your things! Don't just stand there, you whore bitch of your whoring mother! Collect your filthy things and take them over there to the canning shed!"

The sun beat with ferocity on the hard dirt of the courtyard.

"No," Jim said. "She stays in the house."

Cornelius shook with indignation. He was about to object.

"Not a word, Cornelius," Jim said. "*Váyate.*"

Cornelius said something under his breath to

Jewel in the local dialect. He turned and walked slowly across the yard toward the canning shed, P'en trailing behind like a cat on a leash.

Jim glanced up from the glass he was shining and saw Nick trudging his way through the sea grape–covered dunes from the beach.

Jim had completely forgotten about the weird incident with Heather at the bar the night before, and he prayed Nick wasn't coming to blame his wife's wandering eye on Jim. His simple resort life had all of a sudden become embroiled with conflict, and he didn't want more.

"How about another knockout Bloody Mary?" Nick said affably. "I need to make certain yesterday wasn't just a fluke."

"Right away," Jim said, relieved.

"You make a hell of a Bloody."

"Learned it from a friend. This is his special recipe."

As Jim mixed the drink, he thought about Iraq, wondered what would have happened if he'd never deployed. He would have never met K-Tell or learned how to make a Bloody. He would have been a regular cop rather than an SRO, and he'd have never met Malinda and lost her. He would have never lost himself, cowering behind the red steel door outside the cafeteria while Kevin White was still shooting.

Thock-thock-thock.

Jim drowned the faraway sound of the Black Hawks by shoving a celery stalk into the Bloody Mary and slid the glass across the counter.

"Wow, this is good," Nick said. "Even better than I remember it."

"Thanks," Jim said. His nerves began to settle.

"You hear about the brouhaha last night?"

And then just like that he was on edge again. *Here it comes*, Jim thought. He wiped the bar.

He didn't want to hear it, but Nick was going to tell him anyway.

"Some guys were up there poking around the casitas."

"Sorry?" Jim blurted in surprise. "Some guys were up where?"

"There were some dudes, and not nice-looking guys either, up nosing around the casitas."

"Who saw them?" Jim asked.

"Heather," he said. "My . . . whatever. She went to bed early. She caught them peeping into the windows of one of the casitas. Perverts. I guess they're everywhere. Anyway, she got into it with them. She's a pistol. For a minute, she said, she was afraid they were going to do something to her."

"Did they try anything?" Jim asked.

Nick took another long swallow from his tall drink with the ground Mayan spices on the rim. "What is this red stuff on here? Paprika? Some other spice?"

"Local stuff," Jim said. "I don't even know the names of half of it."

Nick licked his lips appreciatively, then went on. "She's a tough lady. Doesn't scare easy."

"Yeah," Jim said. "Okay."

"They took off after she confronted them. I know Mexico has problems with drugs and cartels and stuff, but at a place like this?"

"Did you tell the resort director? Antonio?"

"Sure as hell, I did," Nick said. "He said he'd look into it. But what's *he* going to do? I looked around this morning. I didn't see anybody, but there were footprints in the sand back there behind the casitas."

"Did she, Heather, say how many?" Jim asked. "You said there were guys. Plural."

"Three, I think she said."

"Any sign of them after?"

"Nope. They must have kicked it out of there."

And come directly to the station house, Jim thought, but he kept that to himself. "I didn't see anything after I closed up," he told Nick. "Seemed quiet to me."

Nick nodded in agreement. With the Bloody Mary in him, it looked as if his mood had improved.

"There's a lot of secrets in the place, I think," he said, setting his empty glass on the bar. "A lot of mystery. The ruins, the crazy church back there with no furniture and the giant cross wrapped in purple fabric. It's really trippy stuff."

"Another Bloody?" Jim asked.

"They certainly make you want more than one," Nick said. "Give it to me in a roadie, though. I want to go down to the beach."

Jim poured from the shaker into a tall acrylic glass with the resort logo on it.

"Cheers," Nick said.

"*Salud.*" Jim put two ticks on the Dimitriou

chit as he watched Nick stroll past the pool and down the path to the quiet beach.

As dusk was beginning to fall, Héctor came out from the service area, pushing a drinks trolley. Once a week he made balché for curious resort guests. Not authentic balché, of course—that was both too sacred and too potent to be served without the threat of all hell breaking loose. But a fanciful facsimile made the guests feel like they were getting a taste of the region, and the drinks were a hot ticket.

Héctor pulled up at the bar and began collecting supplies. As he loaded the trolley, he peered at Jim. "You okay, boss?"

"How do you mean, amigo?"

"I mean, I bumped into Jewel and I heard about what went down last night. You don't look hurt, but I know how below-the-neck hits can be hidden with a guayabera."

Jim fingered his ribs through his loose white shirt and chuckled, which led to a grimace. "Yeah, I've felt better. But I don't think anything's broken. I'll be fine." He regarded his friend with a worried look. "What happens next, Héctor?"

Héctor paused. He focused on the cart and tapped one of the bottles, its bright pink contents a mystery to Jim. "What happens next is I make some drinks. Then the gringos have a story to tell back home. How they drank balché made by a real live *indio*." He held out his arms and struck a pose to show off his balché trolley costume, a colored serape and a flat-topped Panama like the villagers in the interior wore.

Jim grinned. "I mean about last night."

Héctor nodded. "It's a bad thing, jefe. No doubt about it. In lots of ways."

"We need to talk to Yax Pakal."

"A few of his men came by already, to check up on us."

"What did they say?"

"That Sherif Ali is up to something new. They said, for sure, something bad is coming."

"How bad? Is Yax Pakal up to it?" Jim asked. "Do you think he can handle these thugs?"

Héctor looked thoughtful. "Yax Pakal is a tough hombre. Tough as this *cabrón* from up north, I'm sure of it. But it's going to get ugly. This is war, I think."

"War," Jim repeated, and the sound of the word summoned the *thock-thock-thock* of a Black Hawk. Jim closed his eyes to drown it out, opening them only when he was thinking clearly again. "Drugs."

"It's more than drugs, boss. This is stuff that goes way back. This is jungle stuff. These guys are fighting battles we don't even see. Me, a Mexican, an hombre who has been around a long time and seen a lot—it doesn't all add up even to me. My bosses don't understand. *Your* bosses don't understand."

"What's there to it beyond just cartels muscling in on this territory?"

Héctor whistled, long and low. "You've had a good run down here, boss. When Señor Marlow called me, I said, sure, it's quiet here. Send him down. Let him lick some wounds down here in the sun. Get himself back together. Sure. And you have a good time, no? You get yourself together real good. But it's not your war. What happened last night? It shouldn't have been you. If you wanted to move on—"

"I'm not done here, Héctor," Jim interjected. "I've run from my failures before, and I'm done running."

"Don't you get yourself involved, boss."

"I already am, aren't I, Héctor?"

"Listen, boss, if this weren't my home, I'd move on, too. This place is going to get hot as a pistol. There's too much going on. Too many people involved. Stuff none of us understand."

"All the more reason for me to stay, then."

"Jefe," Héctor pleaded.

"Amigo," Jim said. "Last night I felt something I haven't for a long, long time. I'm not looking for a fight, believe me. I've seen enough for a lifetime. But I'm not walking on you. Or your wife or Sammy. Or this place. Or Jewel. Not this time. I'm not."

Héctor sighed and resumed setting up the trolley. As he filled a five-gallon bucket with ice, he said, "This isn't your fight, boss," trying to persuade Jim one last time. "This thing goes way back. It's a Mexican thing. It's a Conquista thing. These guys, they have been fighting each other since Jesus himself was a baby."

"After last night, it's my fight, too."

Héctor held out his hands in resignation. "Okay, boss, whatever you say."

"By the way, you hear anything about some men poking around out by the casitas last night?"

"Antonio told me."

"I guess they must have been the same guys who came for me," Jim said.

"I think so." Héctor nodded and grabbed the trolley handle.

Jim straightened and looked down toward the beach. Torches lit the trail through the dunes. "They're coming back, aren't they?" he asked. "Harder."

"Jefe, like I say, these hombres mean business. This is war."

Once again, Jim realized just how far away he was from Gary, Indiana.

Jim was passing through reception the next morning when a raised voice caught his attention, and he found Nick Dimitriou yelling at Antonio.

"We were woken up by this awful ranchero garbage blasting through our windows at two a.m. This place is supposed to be off-grid. If I wanted Mexican music, I could go to East LA!"

Antonio was listening intently, doing his best to keep the horror from showing on his face.

"Then I see one of them outside the window of my casita," Nick went on. "*Peeing!*"

"Peeing?" Antonio asked, his expression now stricken.

"Yes, *peeing!*" Nick repeated. "My . . . wife was inside and some dude was taking a piss on the side of our casita."

Antonio's cheeks reddened, and he fiddled with a pen as though taking notes on the problem might make it go away.

"Then another goon came over and he put his face right up to the window," Nick said. "When he saw me, he gave a smarmy leer. This is too damn much."

"This is—er, obviously—it, it goes without saying," stammered Antonio, trying to remain calm, "extraordinary behavior."

"*Extraordinary?*" said Nick. He looked like he was building up to something dramatic. "The only things that should be *extraordinary* around here are the food and the service. Obscene behavior by . . . Mexicans should not be on that list! Fix it!"

"Señor, please, this is a very difficult situation," Antonio pleaded.

"Fix it," Nick repeated firmly, then turned and noticed Jim. "Hey, bartender!" he called amiably, changing mood entirely. "This day could really use another of your amazing Bloodys. Can you hook me up?"

Jim was taken aback by Nick's sudden shift and wondered if his acting skills might be greater than Jim had given him credit for.

Later that afternoon, Antonio came into Bar Balché and stormed over to the bar.

"You know the people in the Tamal casita?" he asked Jim.

Jim nodded. They were a wealthy couple from Vancouver named Liu. Multiple-repeat, elite guests. "Sure," he said.

"They're mad as hell." Antonio plopped onto a stool and sighed. "Mr. Liu says he's got Mr. Klopp's cell phone number."

"I doubt that," Jim said. "What happened?'

"The wife ran into two drunk outsiders when she was returning to her casita. They started giving her trouble. One got handsy with her."

"No way," Jim said.

"I'm afraid so. Her husband heard the commotion and came out. The men started making cat's eyes, saying *Chinita* this, *Chinita* that. Then one grabbed his crotch and gyrated at Mrs. Liu before they pranced off laughing."

Jim shook his head in disbelief.

"It's Los Siguientes," Antonio said, cupping

his face in his hands and massaging his forehead. "I don't know what to do."

The situation came to a head the next day. When
Jim entered the resort's tiled reception area that
morning, he found Héctor and Antonio waiting for him. The breeze, as fresh as always, lifted the palm frond fringe that surrounded the
sleek space.

"Hey, boss," Héctor said. "We got something
to talk about."

From Héctor's serious tone, Jim knew there
could only be one topic to discuss, but he kept
his own response casual. "What's up, hombre?
Hey, Antonio."

Antonio was staring down at the counter,
turning sheets in a client file back and forth.
He looked up and cleared his throat. "We got
another 'message' from Cancún," he said. "In
the form of an 'invitation.' For me to go up

there for a couple of days and get to meet the 'locals.'"

"Say no," Jim scoffed. "Tell them to go to hell."

Antonio merely shuddered.

"Thing is, boss," Héctor cut in, "and let me please explain, these guys have a way they do things. By 'inviting' us, they are offering a negotiation. A sit-down. Yeah, sure, we're not going to go for it, but there's a method to it all. It's a sign of respect. It shows they're not sure who they're dealing with. On which side who is who. You see, no respect would be: They come down here and shoot up the place and maybe kill some people to send a message. But they don't know us yet. Maybe they're a little scared. Maybe they offer something."

Jim couldn't believe it. "There's nothing," he said, "*nothing* a bunch of cartel thugs have to offer. Besides, they haven't exactly left us in peace. What about the Peeping Toms outside the casitas, and what they did to poor Mrs. Liu? Not to mention the visit they already paid me. Is this what they meant by 'You have three days'? Three days until they expect us to give in?"

"*Sí*, yes, I get it, Jim," Héctor said. "But, you know, they didn't come down and shoot us up and maybe kill some people. The way they see it, they've already been, you know, *gracioso*. So, the thing is this: We do nothing and then they come down and shoot us up and kill some people because they feel, again, you know, *irrespetado*. Doing nothing, well, it ain't an option now that they talked to us."

"Why don't we call the main office? Grupo Klopp? They don't want this shit going down on one of their properties."

Antonio exchanged a look with Héctor, who gave a slight nod of assent, before responding. "We tried that. Sherif Ali and his thugs. They threatened us. Before you got here. Set fire to one of the cabanas. It was empty, but they didn't know that. We got lucky. And we got the message. We're on our own here."

Jim knew that if Héctor was correct, and he always was, especially about this stuff, somebody had to make good on the offer to visit Cancún. If Antonio went, however, it was as good as sending nobody at all. Antonio was a good guy, a nice guy, an *efficient* guy. The slim, courtly gentleman who catered to the whims of Las Posadas's clientele was like the super-butler of some mythical English country house. Amazing at his job, but not exactly a first choice to send into negotiations with a cartel boss.

Jim didn't know about *narcotraficantes*, but at least he'd been inside a combat zone. It wasn't as much as some people made it to be, but it was, under these circumstances, preferable to the product of four semesters at hospitality school in upstate New York.

As he reached his decision, Jim noticed

Antonio wasn't just waiting for a response. He was waiting for *that* response. And in that moment, everything clicked. Jim realized why the two of them had jumped him first thing. And while he didn't know the full reason Marlow had sent him to Altún, he suspected that, if he did, it would have something to do with this.

"You can't go, Antonio," he said. "That would be too obvious. It would look like Las Posadas was capitulating. Like we were officially agreeing to whatever they demanded. Las Posadas needs the proverbial 'measure of deniability.' I'll go. I can talk the talk and whatever happens, we can say it didn't."

Antonio nodded, the slightest glimmer of relief smoothing his brow, going along with the façade that this was Jim's idea.

"Problem is, though," Jim said, turning to Héctor, "you've got to come, too. I can't get around up there on my own. I don't know enough. I've got to have a guide."

"Okay, boss," Héctor said readily. "You say so. We leave *mañana*."

Tomorrow. Jim wondered what he was getting himself into. And he wondered if this was why Chuck Marlow had included the loaded Beretta 9mm in a well-oiled holster in the envelope he'd given him when he left Indiana.

Jim and Jewel ate their midday meal in silence. Jim tried to savor the juicy *caldo de pollo* with lime and fresh tortillas stuffed with shaved and spiced turkey, fried, and served with a tomatillo sauce, but his mind was anywhere but the meal. The danger ahead weighed on both their nerves.

"Is there a local *policía*?" Jim asked, breaking their silence.

"There aren't *policía* here," she said. "The closest cops are in Chetumal. The only law here is the *batab*, Yax Pakal."

"And what about *Federales*?"

"The soldiers don't come here, either," Jewel said. "When they do, they disappear. So they don't come to the jungle. This is stuff that goes back generations."

"How so? Drugs? Corruption?"

"Further than that, even. Back to the beginning. Before the beginning, really. Before the conquest, the people in the Balam were in decline. Years, maybe centuries, of feuding between cities had depleted the wealth of everyone. Up north, those people, the Serpent people, the Aztecs as you gringos say, had become ascendent. They were nibbling away at the periphery of the empire. But the Aztecs were mountain and plains people. When they came to the lowland jungles, their conquests slowed. Still, the Balam continued to decline.

"Then came the Spaniards. Because the gold by that point was rumored to be up north, and that was certainly where the wealth was, they headed that direction, toward Mexico. Next, they turned south, toward Guatemala. The fact was, the Spanish never did 'conquer' the Yucatán, at least not in the way they did the rest of Mexico. They let it be. The padres came and the church came, but the authorities left the Yucatán alone. Sure, around Mérida there were the great haciendas, run by wealthy families. But in the Balam the people were left on their own.

"After the independence, the authorities began to worry about the Balam. Santa Ana began a war that lasted eighty years. In the end things were hardly more resolved than when they began. In some ways, things have not changed. The Mexicans control the Yucatán, certainly in the north and the resorts. But down here, in the Balam? They are their own people, with their own laws. And after so many years of fighting with nothing but loss and death to show, the government has little interest in interfering."

She paused for a minute and took another bite of fried tortilla before continuing.

"No one, not the Yucatán police or the national force or even the army, will come here. The days are not so far gone that a guero from the north to be caught in the Balam was to be killed on sight and without question."

Jim's stomach suddenly felt full of rocks rather than lunch. He had understood why Sherif Ali's thug had told him to leave. But now he saw why Jewel had encouraged him to go, too. He was a gringo. In a fight between the people and the outsiders, the continuation of a battle from time immemorial, a gringo would be little more than a lateral casualty.

As Jim's stomach roiled, Jewel casually finished off the last tortilla and wiped her fingers on a napkin. "We're on our own."

11

Sherif Ali was a former street tough. As a child he ran drugs in a tough neighborhood on the east side of Guadalajara. When a Sinaloa cartel muscled in, Sherif Ali continued working but now for the new overlords. At the birthday when he aged out of being a runner, he was inducted into the cartel's hit squad. It was the natural next step on a career trajectory that likely wouldn't see him live past twenty-five.

As a young man, he was ruthless and economical in the execution of his duties. The Sinaloans gave way to the stronger Sonorans, and Sherif Ali got moved, first to Nuevo Laredo and then to Juarez. Despite the constant slaughters and coups and, sometimes, mergers, Sherif Ali survived. He rose up the ranks in each cartel for which he labored. And when a splinter group of the Sonorans, called Los Siguientes, assassinated five men in an hour on a dirt street in Chihuahua, Sherif Ali found himself promoted again.

For his many years of loyal and ruthless service the new directorate rewarded him with a profitable territory, the Yucatán. His instructions were to consolidate the holdings of the cartel. It was a mop-up operation, essentially, following the bloody conquests of Los Ojos, one of the cartels Los Siguientes had consumed.

Sherif Ali inherited a well-run operation. Los Ojos had invested their profits in real estate. Via the usual rat maze of shell companies, Sherif Ali arrived to find himself director of a resort in the Hotel Zone in Cancún.

With his position came a key card to a

rooftop suite at the Hotel Imperador, a cadre of loyal enforcers, and a distribution network worth hundreds of millions of U.S. dollars, just from narcotics sales from Cancún and down the Riviera Maya. The network came with the usual headaches and dangers. The rooftop suite came with its own swimming pool and panoramic views of the Caribbean.

Sherif Ali enjoyed the fruits of his labors. His crew was made up mostly of local toughs, hard men who had few options. They all had one or more family members who worked a job in the Hotel Zone.

Sherif Ali was a comically small man with a violent temper. His first lieutenant was a large man with a violent temper and a huge appetite for mayhem. He was known as El Fofo. The two men had been together since the killing days in Tonalá, outside Guadalajara. A fraternal bond might have existed between them, had either of them the capacity for feeling.

Mostly Sherif Ali lounged beside his private pool in the company of his cadre and kept track of his cash on a laptop following the ever-changing numbers on a spreadsheet. His men kept the pool adorned with a supply of scantily clad international tourists his men trolled from the beaches below. There were plenty to choose from. In the jetsam of such huge resorts were an array of women who had been left behind by one junket or another. They lived by their "wits and tits," as one once said. They were not professionals, but the routine of their lives was largely indistinguishable from that of those who were.

That Saturday, the harem corps consisted of a Canadian, a German, and a Russian, who hated the German but thought the Canadian was her friend. All three were pretty and young. The German had been in residence the longest, catering as she did to some dark need Sherif Ali had only just recently discovered in himself.

The Canadian had been around the pool nearly as long, while the Russian was the newest arrival. She was from the farthest reaches of the Russian Far East and had gone on a Mexican bender only to find she had missed the kleptocrat's return flight to Moscow. All three women lounged topless beside the pool.

They had only Sherif Ali to serve. El Fofo kept them in line but also kept an eye on his men. Nothing could lead to the rightly feared "drive to the cenote" faster than tampering with one of Sherif Ali's women.

Jim would have been astonished by the Hotel Imperador's opulence had he not spent the past many months catering to the guests at the equally posh Las Posadas. One thing this resort did have over Las Posadas was height, and Jim's stomach lurched just a tad as he and Héctor were escorted to the rooftop suite, though he wasn't sure if it was from the elevator ride or the knowledge of who he'd find at the end of it.

He steeled himself as the doors began to slide open, but he was still not prepared for the sight that met them. Three stunningly gorgeous women lounged topless beside a crystal pool, so intent upon their sunbathing that they didn't seem to notice the men's arrival. Jim sucked in a surprised breath before the green-uniformed bellman pointed to a large table beneath a palm-fronded pergola. Jim and Héctor crossed the tiled deck to the shade of the covered table.

A short and wiry man with a comical mustache and closely cropped hair greeted them enthusiastically. "Sit, hombres, sit yourselves. *Mucho gusto, mucho gusto,*" he said, shaking first Héctor's hand and then Jim's. "I am Sherif Ali."

Jim eyed the man warily. He wore aviator sunglasses, which were too large for his head. His unbuttoned linen shirt and designer jeans had a sort of camp showiness, as if he had dressed to impress a Soviet, which perhaps he had.

Behind him loomed a large man wearing a cowboy shirt. The slightest sneer widened his lips when he looked at Jim, and that was all it took for Jim to recognize his attacker from a few days ago. Jim crossed his arms in defiance, and perhaps protection, but when Sherif Ali sat at the table, his henchman folded into a chair along the perimeter, and Jim eased his stance as he and Héctor joined their host at the table.

Two white-shirted servants hustled out to the pergola, one carrying a tray and the other a stand, and they bustled around the table distributing glasses of ice, bottles of Fanta, and a fifth of añejo tequila.

Sherif Ali himself poured each of their glasses half full of tequila, then topped them off with orange Fanta. He held his glass aloft, and first Héctor and then Jim followed suit.

"Amigos, I am very glad to welcome you here

to the Hotel Imperador," the small man said. "It is the finest, I think you will find, of all the fine hotels along this beach of Cancún. Next door, there is the Four Seasons. On the other side, you will find a Ritz-Carlton. Of the three, this is the best. Everybody says so. And—you can imagine, amigos!—the person who can afford to stay in all three, he must have discriminating taste!"

And this, thought Jim, *is the intimidating Sherif Ali.*

"You will stay, you will see. You will eat at our most famous restaurant. You will go to the disco and dance. You will meet the most beautiful women of Mexico. You will see, my friends, my guests! You will see."

Héctor finished his drink and poured himself another. It was a gesture Sherif Ali studied.

"To what," said Héctor, following a big gulp

of his concoction, "do we owe your hospitality, señor?"

"It is a gesture of conviviality, *mi amigo*. You, too, are in the business of hospitality, no? We are colleagues in that respect. What is good for me is good for you as well. And all of this"— Sherif Ali spread his arms apart theatrically; somehow, an unlit cigar had appeared in his left hand—"all of this we share. The beach, the sea, the muchachas, and the money! There is plenty for everyone. There is plenty, don't you agree, Don Héctor, for all to share?"

Héctor tipped his head philosophically. It was unlikely they had been summoned to Cancún to discuss sharing.

"Let me tell you a story," Sherif Ali continued. "This is not my only, you know, business. *Negócio*, *sí*? I have other interests in and around the area. One of these, of them, this is the business of, let's say, *farmacéuticas*. This you do not do, no? No, I did not think so. *Bueno*. In this thing we share"—again he swung a cigar-holding arm— "we each have a bit of the plenty given to us by God. Agreed. But in the other? Much different. You do no business. I do much business. And in this business is a limited resource. It is not like the sun and the sea and the sand and the muchachas. It is much more limited. The resources are much poorer. But this is of no matter. Because you, my friends, you have no interest in these matters."

Jim could feel the sweat begin to trickle down his back.

"So, to where we come. There are people, no, I should say, there is a person, a certain person of your region who causes me, 'ay, Señor.'" Sherif Ali theatrically smacked his cigar-holding palm against the crown of his head. "This hombre, this *cabrón*, he know from *cabrón, sí?*" Sherif Ali nodded toward Jim. "*Sí*. This *pinche cabrón*, he try and take what is mine in your area. He is, what do they say in English? The little worm

that suck your blood in the water. He is one of
those maggots, insects, filthy pests. He is *indio*.
Not even a man of God! They laugh at *nuestro
padre*, you know? Laugh!"

"You mean Yax Pakal," Héctor said.

"Ay," Sherif Ali said again, waving his palm
before his eyes as if chasing off a massive mos-
quito. "*Exactamente*. This one. This guy. He's
down there, in that *pinche* jungle and giving us
all the grief. He is taking business that is ours.
He is not listening to our reason."

"Have you spoken with him?" Héctor asked.

"No. What does a man like me, a business-
man, talk to no *pinche indio* for? No," Sherif
Ali said. "That *pendejo* down there isn't paying
us what he owes."

"And what would you like for us to do in this,
señor?" Héctor asked.

"Nothing! Nothing at all! Enjoy yourselves.
Stay at my hotel here."

"And?"

"In some time, sometime soon, I believe, some men will come down to where you are for business. They will deal with this sucker blood, this vampire *indio*. I am merely performing here, *mis amigos*, the generosity of letting you know a few of my associates will be visiting. They will not bother you. They will be there only to see this man."

Jim finally decided to speak up. "Yax Pakal and his people are good and honest people. These *indigenas* who follow Yax Pakal, I don't think they will appreciate being dictated to by your associates."

Sherif Ali looked at Jim as if he'd just recognized his presence. "Señor," he said. "Don Jaime, if I may. This man"—he gestured to his left to Héctor—"has been in this place for many, many years. You, I think, have been only a little. Not even one year."

"You haven't been around so long yourself," Jim said. "Appearances notwithstanding."

"You work for that hotel, yes? Las Posadas?"

"I do," Jim said.

"And you are here because . . . ?"

"Because you invited us," Jim said.

"No, señor, respectfully. I invited Don Héctor and Don Antonio, the man who is your *director*."

"Well," Jim said, "you got me instead."

"It is a nice place, Las Posadas, would you say, yes?"

"It's a very nice place," Jim said. "Very nice."

"And you have there, what do you say, the movie stars and models and rich computer guys from California?"

"It's an elite clientele," Jim said.

"So, señor, you have this very nice place, *sí*? And you have these fancy people, very rich, very important, who come to your resort, to Las Posadas?"

Jim said nothing. Héctor remained impassive next to him, though Jim could see his thighs beginning to flex, like he might leap from his chair and barge away in disgust at any moment.

"But you are down there, no? All the way down in this *pinche* little town called Altún. Many kilometers from any city. Many kilometers from any police or fire or any of those things. You are very remote, I think?"

"The remoteness is the attraction," Jim said.

"Should something happen, though, señor. As a fellow innkeeper, I can share your anxieties. What should happen, say, if there be a disaster of some sort. A fire. Or, *Dios mío,* no, some killing or something like that? You would be very much alone, I think."

"We take care of ourselves," Jim said.

"You would sleep easier tonight, I think, if you knew you were safe, señor. Safe from the dangers."

Jim looked around the deck of the penthouse. The three women wearing nothing but dental floss still lay motionless by the pool. There

were two modernist blocks beyond them, presumably penthouse suites, and on the bayside
a white screen hid the building machinery. On
the ocean side, the Caribbean ran from emerald
to aquamarine to sapphire, like a good tropical
ocean should. At the far end of the deck, three
toughs lounged on resort furniture around a
low glass table. All three wore shoulder holsters.

Jim returned his gaze to Sherif Ali and noticed the massive man behind him sit up a little
straighter, coiled for action.

Sensing the tension, Sherif Ali smirked.
"Something eat your tongue there, Don Jaime?"
He glanced back and acted surprised to find
the bigger man behind him. "Oh, my apologies,
sénors, I forgot to introduce you to El Fofo.
But, I think, maybe you met before?" His expression danced between innocence and guile.

Héctor drained his glass and stood from the
table. "When are you thinking you will return

the visit, amigo?" he asked, as Jim pushed his own chair back and stepped to Héctor's side.

"*No sé*," Sherif Ali said.

Then he rose as well and narrowed his eyes at Jim. "Listen to me, *mi amigo*, this is what I brought you here to say. You have three choices before you. Three choices, one of which to make. See how generous is Sherif Ali? He's giving you choices for you to make!"

"I don't care for any of your choices," Jim replied with a contemptuous glare.

"Listen good, amigo. I only tell you once. First, you may join me. Look around you. Pretty girls. Plenty to eat and drink. Everybody does good who goes with Sherif Ali."

Jim glared harder.

"Second, you may run. I give you a very nice head start. Leave this place, leave Mexico. Go back to your stinking town up there in the *norte*.

Go back to your family, your friends, where you belong. But go. And go fast. Run."

"And third?"

"And third? You no go with me? You not do the smart thing? I think you're a smart man, *mi amigo*. But you not do what I ask you of?"

"What is the third option," Jim demanded calmly.

"Well, then. Third. Third choice is: You die."

Sherif Ali clapped his hands three times loudly. "Get these two to their rooms!" he barked. "Now!" He lowered a dark and malevolent gaze at Jim. "Get out," Sherif Ali spat.

The bellman rushed over. "Gentlemen," he said. He pointed an arm toward the elevator bank, not meeting their eyes.

"*Buena suerte*," Sherif Ali said dismissively.

Héctor and Jim made a beeline for the elevator, followed by the attendant, who quickly pressed the call button. The doors slid open and the men stepped inside, but instead of closing immediately as expected, the doors clacked back and forth a few times, presumably a glitch in the circuitry. The attendant pressed the button again, without betraying any annoyance, and as they waited, a crashing noise, like that of a table being upended, came from the deck, which was just out of sight. The attendant began punching the button more furiously.

"*'Buena suerte? Buena suerte!'*" a man's voice, most certainly Sherif Ali's, shouted. "This gringo is dead! Fucked! And I should kill all of you, too!" he yelled. "Sitting there like *idiotas. Pendejos!* What happened in Ciudad Juarez should happen to you, you imbeciles! For letting that happen! He called me out!"

There came the scraping of leather soles across the clay tiles of the unseen patio deck.

"*Jesús lloró!*" Sherif Ali shouted. "Holy Mary, mother of God, you *pinche* idiots and babies!"

"*Sí, capitán*," said multiple men's voices in rough unison. "*Sí*, Sherif Ali, jefe."

"*Pinche* idiots. You *pendejo* little girls. We will go down to the fancy place of this fabulous gringo and I will put a bullet in his head! '*Buena suerte*,' I will say then, for the last time!"

The color drained from the face of the elevator attendant and he gave up poking the unresponsive button.

"Russia girl!" they heard Sherif Ali yell. "You! Now!"

With that, as if drawing the curtain on this little drama, the elevator doors finally closed.

"We're not staying, are we?" Jim asked Héctor.

"It's a nice place," Héctor said. "But not nice enough to spend your last night."

When the elevator doors opened on the ground floor, thankfully without another glitch, the pair crossed the lobby at a brisk pace and burst through the entrance to find the Toyota parked nearby. Jim palmed a wad of pesos into the hand of the valet and took the keys, then hopped behind the wheel. He needed the control of driving to help settle his nerves.

They drove in silence for a while and had crossed over the causeway and turned on the coastal highway back toward Altún before Héctor broke it.

"You got pretty salty back there, boss," he said.

"He didn't seem like such a tough guy to me."

"Sure, but you see all those goons he's got? I mean, this guy's a leader in Los Siguientes. These are some bloodthirsty operators."

"Like I said," Jim said. "He didn't look so tough to me."

"Okay, hombre. If you say so."

Jim gripped the wheel. Nothing was in fullness yet, but he could feel the first buds of confidence reappearing inside. It had been a long winter.

12

The next morning, Jim and Jewel were working at the Chapel of San Torcuato, getting some final touch-ups completed before the festival began in two days, when Sammy appeared in the doorway.

"Don Jaime!" he cried, out of breath from having run from Las Posadas.

"*Callate!*" barked Doña Lora, who was crouched in her usual spot beside the Talking Cross with a young mother and her baby. "*Estás en iglesia!*"

"What is it, Sammy?" Jim handed off the sisal rope to one of the men from the village also working the masonry and led the boy outside.

"My father," he blurted. "He says something is come to the hotel that you need to look at."

"Something, Sammy? Or someone?"

"I don't know. It's a thing, I guess. Papa did not say whether it was a thing or a person. But I think a thing would be more interesting."

"Okay, *chico*," Jim said putting out his hand for Sammy to take. "Let's go have a look at this thing."

Sammy pulled on Jim's hand, urging him to run. Jim smiled and began an obliging trot. It was then he saw it. Black smoke billowed into the sky over the resort. Jim let go of Sammy's hand and flew as quickly as possible toward Las Posadas.

Héctor and a stricken Antonio met him in the forecourt. Through the windows of the reception building, he could see the thatched roof of Bar Balché burning furiously, the flames shooting high into the air.

"I've got staff moving guests onto the beach back past the last of the casitas," Antonio said.

"Where's the tanker truck?" Jim asked.

"I called for it!" Antonio cried in anguish. "It should be here!"

"I heard some chatter just before," Héctor said. "When I came out, I thought I saw a couple of those *norteños* running back toward the beach. I sent Sammy to get you, and then I heard a loud pop and rushed out to find this." He shook his head in disbelief.

Jim nodded, wondering for a moment where Sammy had gone, but realizing these distraught men needed leadership. "Héctor, run back to the shed and see what's keeping them with the tanker. Antonio, you'd better clear out whatever's valuable in reception. If the wind shifts, it's going to blow the flames back this way. It will take out reception, too."

Héctor raced off, and Antonio, covering his mouth with worry, hustled inside.

Jim thought he saw movement through the landscaping beyond the burning roof and in the direction of the casitas. Before he had a chance to investigate, the hulking water truck came flying into the drive, jumping up over a curb and busting through the plantings. Héctor rode the running board, gripping the side mirror with both hands.

As the truck's massive load of water sloshed in the tanker, Héctor and three other resort workers unraveled the hoses. One man turned a big red wheel and water began spraying with great force into the burning palm and palapa.

Barely audible over the roar of the water and flames, Jim thought he heard a gunshot come from the direction of the casitas. Héctor moved to hand Jim his hose so he could take the other now readied by the men, but Jim turned instead and ran into the compound.

When he reemerged, the fire had been doused and black muck full of charred straw swam over the paved floor of what had once been Bar Balché. One of the hoses was still going, now trained on the surrounding roofs in the event of any lurking live embers.

In his arms, Jim carried Sammy's limp frame, dead from a single high-caliber shot to the chest. He had found the boy beneath an immature banana plant. The force of the bullet had knocked Sammy's small body off the path to the casitas and into the shrubs.

The plume of water ceased. The three other men, who had been shouting over the spray, fell silent.

Héctor turned to find out why the hose had stopped. Then, seeing the men's expressions, he turned back toward the smoldering building. It was only then he noticed Jim.

Héctor had seen much, done much. For most of his youth he had worked freelance in a business where life could be short and cheap. Mostly, he had been on the good side. Other times, whether any side was good had been hard to discern. He'd retired as far from that world as he could find, married a local woman. She'd born him five children, all girls, whom he'd raised in the safety of Altún. And then came the miracle of Sammy, years younger than his older sisters, most of them by that time with children themselves.

Héctor took the body of his only son from Jim's arms. Without emotion on his face, creased by time and weather and hardship enough already for many lives, he turned and began carrying his little boy toward the village, where his wife, Valeria, was getting ready for the Festival of San Torcuato with the rest of the villagers.

Even though Héctor couldn't possibly have reached his house yet, Jim could almost hear Valeria's keening on the soft wind.

* * *

Jim was sitting in a chair, staring forlornly at the remains of his workplace, when he noticed Cornelius O'Connor, dressed in one of his shabby linen suits, waddle into the courtyard. His hands were clasped behind his back, forcing his broad gut outward even farther. He appeared to be studying the wreckage.

Jim approached the portly man. "If I find out," he said, then stopped. "I know you're involved, Cornelius, though I'd be wrong to give you much credit. But you're involved, I know it. And now you've got Sammy's blood on your hands."

Cornelius drew himself up to his full, if pitiable, height. He puffed out his chest and tried to strike a pose of importance.

"What are you doing here, Cornelius?" Jim asked with exasperation.

Cornelius gave him a long and imperious

look. "I am here to assess the damage," he said finally, "so as to share a report with my colleagues."

"Your *colleagues*, Cornelius?"

Cornelius merely shrugged and frowned. As if he were somehow unaffected. "I, too, have a proper role as the former station chief," he said. "I plan to execute it."

"Your next berth isn't going to be the cannery, Cornelius. Not if I have any say."

"Your threats are idle," Cornelius said, half turning away.

"Just get out."

The small man took off his hat and wiped his nut-brown bald head with a handkerchief.

"You don't know who you're dealing with, Mr. Lord. The tables have changed. The wind blows now from the north. You'll pay for your insolence. You will pay with your worthless life!"

"Go. Now!"

Someone else might pay with their life, all

right, and Jim desperately hoped it would be a snake like Cornelius rather than him.

The surface of the swimming pool rippled in a slight breeze. Bits of charred thatch floated on the blue. Jim inspected what up until an hour ago had been Bar Balché. Everything was gone. It had burned down to the limestone blocks on which it had stood.

"Joven!" a voice called.

Jim looked up. At the far end of the terrace a man sat alone at a table beneath an umbrella. Smoke blurred Jim's view, but through the smell of destruction he was quickly able to decipher the figure.

It was Sherif Ali.

On his head he wore an expensive and pristine cowboy hat. His guayabera was clean and pressed.

Jim walked slowly toward him.

"Ah, señor," Sherif Ali said. "So good to see you again."

No one else was on the deck, and Jim couldn't see anyone behind him or on the path to the sea.

"Please, please," Sherif Ali said. He gestured toward the empty chair at the table. "Join me."

Jim sat.

"So, we meet again so soon," Sherif Ali said. "Tell me, what was it you did not like about my offer of hospitality? Did you not like your room? Something about the food? Was the girls not to your liking?"

"I didn't stay long enough to see any of that."

"That is a shame, Señor Lord. I think you would have changed your mind."

"I thought I made things plenty clear before. I won't be intimidated. I want you out of here."

"What? After what I did for you, there is not reciprocity?"

"I want you and whoever brought you here out. Get your trucks and go."

"But, señor," Sherif Ali objected, leaning back and linking his hands behind his head. "I am here for the vacation!"

"A boy is dead because of you and your thuggery," Jim said, his voice rising. "Your infantile act of machismo."

"Machismo, señor?" Sherif Ali smiled. "Do not mistake this for machismo." He clenched a fist. "This is pure power, señor. And I will flex it again until this whole place is burned to the ground!"

Jim said nothing. Sherif Ali relaxed his fist.

"The people here, they are very proud of their *pinche* ruins, aren't they?" the cartel boss continued. "The way they cart their saint around, like they aren't all just a bunch of Godless *indios*. But these *pinche* jungles here. They swallowed it all, didn't they? The pyramids and their pools for throwing in the little girls. There is nothing left but *pinche* jungle and *pinche* vines."

"It was once a great civilization."

"You say? He say? This *pinche* jungle tell you that?"

Jim was again silent.

Sherif Ali laughed. "Jim, oh, Jim. You're a funny guy. But these virgins . . ." He waved his hand in the air. "They still have the virgins, don't they, Jim? The beautiful virgins who carry the secrets of these people."

"Get out."

As if on cue, El Fofo arrived and stood behind Sherif Ali's chair.

"Listen, amigo," Sherif Ali said. "A whole big lot will change tomorrow. You see, it is now like this. I am going to take this town for myself. It is going to be Sherif Ali's town. All those villagers? They're maggots, just like him, my friend, and my big boots will crush the life out of them and bring even more death to their precious ruins. And this little place here? Your boss's place? This will now be Sherif Ali's place.

I make it my own. If you like, Jim, I will now be your boss."

"The hell you will."

Sherif Ali smacked his lips. He looked out toward the ocean, the beauty of which clearly had not even a passing effect. He then cast a bland glance around the grounds.

"This is all such a shame," he said. "Could have been avoided, you know? Nobody hurt. Nothing ruined."

For a moment, Jim almost thought he was being reflective.

"But probably," he continued, "you and the other *pinche* idiots and all these *indios* and your whore-faced girlfriend—you never would have understood. You would have manufactured some reason to be angry or to be disloyal or to cheat me. This is the way with you gringos. Boy Scout on the outside, *pinche cabrón* lying cheater in the heart. Ah, well. You've made your choice."

Jim stood and looked down at the malevolent character before him so utterly without
shame or scruples or, it appeared, fear. "Fuck
you," he said. "This is my hotel, not yours."

"Go kiss your whore goodbye," Sherif Ali
said. "This much I give you."

13

That evening in the village, everyone prepared for the festivities. It was the Eve of San Torcuato's Day.

They would all gather at the church for a procession to carry the statue of San Torcuato on a bier to the ruins. There, the holy icon would be placed on a platform atop the tower. After the father said a Mass, a selected group of young men would light a fire and spend the night guarding the saint. The rest of the villagers would return to their street for a communal feast and then rise again early the next morning to repeat the procession in reverse.

Whether San Torcuato was meant to show

ascendency over the ancient ruin, or whether the ancient ruin was there to accept San
Torcuato, it did not matter to the worshipful.
In their hearts, both worlds were one. The
mystery of San Torcuato and his promise and
prophecy blended seamlessly into the more ancient beliefs and traditions.

The day's ritual was unwritten but largely
unvaried over many years. When the sun was
about three-quarters through its downward arc
into the west, the village women met outside
the small house of Doña Lora, the healer. She
sat waiting, her legs crossed on the threshold
of her hut, and blessed the procession. From
there the women marched to the village bak-
ery, where everyone took a bite of pan dulce,
the food of the gods. Next, they stopped at the
Bar Caiman, the hut that served as the social
club for the village men. The men were ready,
carrying the elaborately glazed clay jugs of li-
bations. Mostly they contained balché, though

there were also other stranger and more potent concoctions, which had been brewed exclusively for the most important festival of the year. The final stop was at the schoolhouse, where the children had gathered with the two women who taught each grade and every subject.

There was one notable absence, of course. Sammy Yañez. He had hoped to one day be selected for the saint's special guard. Instead, he was lying on the floor of his parents' hut draped with a white sheet, four candles marking a perimeter around his small body.

The entire village now together, they came by the house to pay their respects to the boy and offer condolences to Héctor and Valeria. Normally they would have come in smaller groups, stayed longer to mourn. But on that auspicious day, the Yañezes broke custom and Valeria joined the rest of her people for the procession to the Chapel of San Torcuato.

When the group arrived, two acolytes, dressed

in white, drew open the doors. The stone floor, constructed from blocks taken from parts of the ruins that were no longer standing, had been swept clean. Tripod censers filled with fragrant copal burned on either side of the great Talking Cross, which was wrapped in fresh purple woven cloth. Just inside the door stood the statue of the saint, taken from its place of privilege on the altar, robed in white with blue trim and a crown of hammered gold, and resting on the ceremonial bier on which it would be carried to the tower.

Still outside, the procession of villagers split into two lines. From the rear approached the six young men who held the honor that year of bearing the saint. Each crossed himself and knelt before the statue before assuming his place on one of its sides. Then the priest emerged, his hands clutching a black rosary and a black missal and clasped behind his back. He was dressed in a black hassock but wore on his shoulders a mantle of indigenous weaving. He drew the missal in front of him, opened it to a page he had long since memorized, and recited a prayer. The villagers responded, Valeria's voice faltering with tears. Then, closing the missal and lowering it and the rosary to his side, the priest raised his face to the dusky sky. He spoke in the native dialect, alternately orating and singing. The people responded again, also in the dialect, also in song.

The priest returned to his missal and while reading, began walking forward. The men inside the chapel raised the bier to their shoulders and, once steadied, followed, the saint aloft between them. They passed through the assembled villagers, who fell in behind, silently. The trek to the ruins had begun.

While the villagers were assembling and preparing to honor San Torcuato, Jim and Héctor waited at the airstrip in the nearby tiny town of Xcalak, which serviced the resort. Soon they heard the drone of a plane and saw a glint of metal in the sky. The speck grew into the discernable shape of a single-engine plane as it dropped down and flew low along the length of the runway. At the far apron it rose again, disappearing briefly into the coral-colored haze before it returned and approached lower still. Far down the strip, a puff of white appeared as the plane touched down onto the oil-slicked runway.

The plane bounced toward them on the roughly maintained surface, slowing and then turning onto the brief taxiway that led to the small tie-down area. The plane was a white Cessna with a red stripe running along its side. The propeller feathered down, and the brakes brought the craft to a halt.

When the prop had ceased turning, the cabin door opened, and Chuck Marlow emerged. He was wearing the same flight jacket as that first day he took Jim flying up the coast to Muskegon and back. In the pulsing tropical heat, the insulated coat quickly became too much. Marlow tore off the jacket, tossing it past the pilot seat and into the cargo hold behind.

"Jim," he said, holding out his hand and taking Jim's in an enthusiastic shake. "I got a text message from our amigo here." He nodded at a somber Héctor who stood a few feet back. "He said this was a good time of year to visit down here."

"Chuck," Jim said, trying to wrap his mind around seeing someone from his old life in his new world, even if it was the person who had sent him there. "This is crazy."

"I know, Jim," Marlow said. "That's why I'm here."

Marlow then strode toward Héctor and the two men embraced long and without words. When they parted, Marlow squeezed his friend's shoulder and the two walked side by side toward the waiting Land Cruiser.

Jim drove them back to the station, where Héctor carried Marlow's small bag up the six blue steps and through the screened door into the house.

Jim and Marlow sank into chairs on the veranda, and Abarrane appeared with two bottles of Montejo. Jim gave Marlow a quick update on the events of the past week while they sipped their beers.

"The thing is," Jim said, "I don't know whether to believe his bluff. Are they just shaking me down by shaking me up? Or does this psycho really believe he can seize Las Posadas? Then what, right? It doesn't make any rational sense."

Marlow wiped his brow with a bandanna and replaced his Panama hat. The cicadas chirped. In the distance, a pod of howler monkeys was getting settled for the night.

"The district police are no help," Jim went

on. "They haven't been around here in thirty years or more. The *Federales* are just as useless."

Marlow remained silent.

"I know what you're thinking," Jim said.

"What's that, Jim?" Marlow asked.

"That I've done it again. That I'm in over my head."

"Well," Marlow said with measure. "You seem better, to begin. Much better than when last I saw you."

"I am," Jim said. "Or I was, but here I am again, right back in it. It's Kevin White all over again. There's a guy who wants to blow the place up, and I don't know how to save it."

"Really?"

"What?" Jim asked. "Is there some easy answer I haven't thought of?"

Marlow smiled ruefully. "There's never an easy answer."

They sat quietly for a few moments, before Jim spoke again. "The past stretches behind us," he began slowly. "I no longer have shame. I'm no longer afraid."

"That's good," Marlow said, his tone kind and almost fatherly. "You're going to need that." He nodded at Jim, then tipped his head to the side. "By the way, I hear that around here they've started calling you *batab*. *Batab* Jim. Lord Jim."

"Oh, that's just chatter." Jim shook his head. "But it's true that this place has changed who I am, Chuck. I'm no longer running. Running from my past, from who I used to be. I feel born anew here." Jim finished his bottle of beer with a long slug. "It was Jewel who changed everything. You'll meet her. She reminds me of Malinda—you'll see it in her, I bet. But she's also so different. She's not of this world." Jim paused. "No, that's not right. That sounds too . . . Let me try again."

"Try what, Jim? People grow. Grow up. Things change. You said it yourself. You don't have anything anymore to apologize for. Sometimes all it takes is time."

"I guess . . . I guess it took me longer than I expected."

"You know, it's not too late, Jim. Nobody would blame you for taking Jewel and getting into that Toyota and driving for a long, long time. Driving until you were way the hell away from here."

"Oh, yeah? What would Mr. Klopp say?"

"He'd say you did the right damn thing. That he'd do the same in your shoes."

"I don't think so. He's got a lot invested here."

"Javier Klopp has a lot invested everywhere. Believe me, I know Javier Klopp. He'd never swap a person for a buck. Not a billion bucks. Believe me."

"It's not just that, Chuck."

"Not just what? You and this woman of yours getting out of here alive?"

"No!" Jim said adamantly. "I ran once. I'm not doing it again."

"You didn't run the first time. You did what any trained soldier would do. This time it's different, anyway. It's a strategic retreat. Live to fight another day."

"You think I would really do that? Retreat? After everything that's happened?"

"Listen, Jim. What happened at Portage was bad. It shouldn't have happened. But you've changed. You're not the same man who was there that day. The world has changed. The *situation* has changed. This?" Marlow waved into the growing darkness. "This isn't your fight, Jim. This isn't your war. This is a territory beef, a drug turf war, a nihilistic battle between forces that don't concern you and never have."

"But they do, Chuck. They do. This is my place now. It's not just about Las Posadas. It's not about Javier Klopp. It's about me. It's about who I've become. I'm not running. And I'm not going back."

The two men heard a creak on the boards of the veranda, and Jewel emerged from the house. Her figure seemed to float toward an empty chair, part of her otherworldliness. There was something always coiled about her, lighter than air but wound down like the nucleus of some impossibly energetic isotope.

Jim watched to see whether Marlow could see her as he did, the way she projected Malinda Murch's luminous ghost.

After brief introductions, Jewel asked the question that hung thick in the air, like the smoke over Bar Balché earlier that day.

"So, what now?"

"Now we find those SOBs and finish this thing once and for all," Jim said fiercely.

Jewel slipped her hand over his and squeezed. "Of course. I guess what I should have asked was how?"

Jim remained silent, pondering the question. "Sherif Ali may have tipped his hand. He said things would change *tomorrow*. What if he meant that literally? What if he's planning an attack tomorrow?"

"It would make sense," Marlow said. "If they're here now, it's because they know about the local traditions. They're going to use the Festival of San Torcuato as a cover or distraction—"

"You're right," Jim interjected, realization sinking in. "Sherif Ali called the villagers insects, said he was going to squash them. I thought he was just talking tough, but he actually means it, doesn't he? He's going to attack the villagers."

Marlow nodded sagely. "It would certainly follow the cartel M.O. Their plan will probably be to kill everybody and make it look political. And then the *Federales* will cover it up. They'll go along with the Siguientes. They don't want people to know the grip the cartel has. Worse, the Siguientes most likely have some of the top guys in their pocket."

"Or they wouldn't have gotten this far . . ." Jim said.

"The government will frame a village attack as an excuse to heighten their presence. And their 'presence' means increased repression of the locals. Nobody in the world would ever know what really happened. This place will have been wiped off the map. Like it never existed."

"We can't let that happen," Jewel said in a fierce whisper. "The people here are just living their lives and not bothering anyone. They don't deserve to die so some drug boss can get even richer."

"That may be," Marlow said softly, "but these guys are ready to fight. And they're here. Somewhere."

"But where?" Jim asked.

"They've pulled back into the jungle or some hidey-hole."

"I don't know, Chuck," Jim said. "There's not a hell of a lot around here. They're not in the village or at the ruins. There's Yax Pakal's place, but they wouldn't be here if they'd already taken him down." He shook his head, a move he was making far more than usual that evening. "You flew over this place, so you know. The rest of it is solid, thick, go-nowhere jungle."

"You'd be surprised what the jungle can hold."

Héctor came out of the house and stepped into the pool of yellow light that encircled Jim, Marlow, and Jewel.

Marlow addressed his old friend. "Who else besides you has a good sense of the land?"

Héctor tipped his head toward the cannery and raised an eyebrow. Jim locked eyes with him and in that instant, he knew.

"Damn him!" he yelled, standing quickly. He ran down the veranda steps and into the dusty yard of the compound. At the cannery, he tore open the door. It was dark inside. No

Cornelius and no P'en. Even Cornelius's hammock had been taken down.

"As I said, the jungle can hide a lot of treachery." Marlow stood in the dust behind him.

"Damn him," Jim repeated, then slammed shut the door to the empty cannery. "Time to game this out."

The procession of villagers behind their venerated saint continued to a steady drumbeat down the churchyard path and into the village. Normally it would have stopped at the edge of town, but this year the group progressed to the Yañez house before pausing, and the platform was lowered to the ground. The people kneeled; the drum stopped. The priest sang another prayer in the local dialect, and a moment of silence followed.

The carriers stood and lifted the saint on his platform again to their shoulders. The people rose, the drum resumed its stately beat, and the procession continued, turning onto the track that led to the pier. There, the same ritual was repeated. The priest stopped, the men lowered their burden, and the procession knelt. Again, the priest turned his face toward the sky and sang his Yucatecan prayer.

This time the men lifted the bier only waist-high to allow the saint to pass through the gates to the ruins. The procession carried on at its reverent pace until the villagers reached the base of the tower. There stood a stone plinth, specially erected for this purpose. On the plinth was a rosewood shelter with a roof of palm fronds. The platform bearers again set their load on the ground.

With deliberate care they laid hands on the statue and, moving together, raised it up onto the plinth within the protective bower. Then they stepped aside.

The villagers behind gathered closely together

around their venerated saint. The priest stepped
forward and raised his crozier. The drumbeat
stopped. A handbell rang. The priest began to
celebrate Mass. He conducted the service entirely in the Yucatecan dialect. His audience
responded aloud at all the appropriate places.
Their attention was complete and intense.

After the communion and the blessing, all
but the six men tasked with guarding the statue began to make their way back toward the
village. What appeared to be every piece of furniture had been brought out to form a snaking
table that ran down the middle of the unpaved
road between the two rows of native houses.
The women hurried into their thatched-roof
homes, while the men took their seats at one
end of the miraculously long table and the
children at the other.

The women began to reemerge, each from
her own kitchen, carrying clay pots and platters
filled with ceviche, beans, chiles rellenos, and

pibil. They set the painted pots and platters all down the table and sat themselves in the middle section between the children and the men. The tavern operator came with his two sons to deliver Presidente brandy, bottles of local beer, and of course the specially prepared balché.

This year, the villagers toasted not only to San Torcuato, but to Sammy Yañez. Valeria sobbed. The feasting began.

14

An hour before dawn, Jim heard the roar of motors and ran out to the compound's edge, where he saw seven black Chevrolet Suburbans speed through the crossroads, banking without braking at the turn that led toward the ruins.

"Son of a . . ." Jim sprinted back to the station house, where Marlow, Jewel, and Héctor sat drinking coffee at the table. "They're on the move."

Marlow grabbed his flight jacket and rose. "It's time to take to the air, then."

Jim nodded as he strapped a holster to his

waist and secured the Beretta in position. The clip was full, and he had a spare in his pocket, but even if every bullet found its target, he might come up short. "Héctor, have we heard back from Yax Pakal?"

Héctor shook his head. "Not yet. I don't know that we will, either. He's either coming or he's not, jefe, and if he does, you'll know it when he gets there." He rose from the table and stepped into the station house, leaving the others to ponder his words for a moment.

Jewel broke the silence. "Abarrane did her part, so the villagers should be ready. It didn't take much convincing, after what happened to Sammy."

Jim nodded solemnly, and Marlow squeezed his shoulder. "You can do this, Jim. Now, do you have the hardware?"

Jim held up a nylon mesh market bag full of crumbling boxes of old rusting nails. "Check!"

Héctor returned from inside, his carbine in hand, a belt with clips at his waist, and a dive knife strapped across his chest.

Marlow gave him an approving once-over. "Héctor, you hold this line as best you can. I don't think they'll come through here, but we can't be sure."

"You got it."

Next to Héctor, Jewel looked vulnerable and small, and Jim's stomach clenched. "Take this machete," he told her, running into his room to snag the weapon, "and barricade yourself in the kitchen. If it's hopeless, we'll come back for you and take the Toyota to the highway."

Jewel took the blade nervously, then reached up and traced her fingers along Jim's jawbone and leaned in so their faces were only inches apart. "Come back to me," she said softly, then touched her lips gently to his, before dashing into the darkness of the station house.

* * *

From atop the tower, San Torcuato's likeness stood watch over Altún. To the north, resort guests were tucked into their lush accommodations, ignorant of the saint's festival and of the plight facing the village. To the south, the villagers bustled about, preparing to bring their saint back to the chapel for a most sacred day.

In the darkness, a line of black Suburbans pulled onto the southern edge of the resort grounds, on the far side of the limestone wall that set off the ruins. Sherif Ali's men exited the vehicles and passed around semi-automatic machine guns, then crept toward the wall and crouched down, awaiting orders.

The lullaby of the surf serenaded the ruins complex. In the stillness, the billy goat let loose a gentle bleat.

**

Jim drove as fast as practicable down the rutted road toward the airstrip at Xcalak, fronds and vines pummeling the Toyota. He parked near Marlow's plane and they sprung out. Marlow used a flashlight to look quickly around the Cessna in a truncated preflight.

"Help me with this," Marlow said over his shoulder. He had taken a key and turned a counter-lock toward the aft. A door to the cargo compartment popped open and after Marlow flipped hasps at each hinge joint, Jim helped him maneuver the cargo door up and out of its hinges. Tilting the hatch, they eased it back into the cargo space. "Where are the flechettes?"

The nails had been Jim's idea, though Marlow was more familiar with the concept. He'd jumped right in with the weapon's history as soon as Jim had suggested using flechettes.

"The French came up with the idea in the

First World War," Marlow had explained to Jewel and Héctor the night before. "They cast these tiny darts, called flechettes, and would drop them by the boatload from their planes over German troops. They were small but heavy enough and sharp enough to cause real damage. And fear. The Americans copied the idea, called it the Lazy Dog bomb. Dropped them by the millions in Korea. Even Vietnam. Caused a lot of grief. Caused a lot of mayhem. A Lazy Dog, if it hit you straight on, had the force of a .45, point blank."

They didn't have any actual vaned darts, but Jim had found a stash of old nails in the cannery that would suffice. Since they were low on manpower and on weapons, the nails would serve as a first strike to reduce the ranks of their enemy. Then Jim would swoop in to take out the rest—and pray that Yax Pakal had indeed received the message and would show up with his jungle army.

Jim handed Marlow the market bag, its plastic handles bent nearly double with the load. Marlow took the boxes out one by one and arranged them in orderly stacks on the floor of the cargo hold. It reminded Jim of the neatness he had glimpsed in Marlow's daybook at Portage High.

Both men climbed into the cockpit, buckled in, and put on the headsets. Marlow cranked the engine, and the prop began its torque. Soon the plane was humming and bouncing as the lift took hold. Marlow cast an owl-like look all around that Jim remembered from flying out of Gary, released the brakes, and eased the craft down the length of the airstrip. He put a hand on the throttle, and they began rolling quickly forward. The missing cargo door made for terrible noise in the cabin. Everything that wasn't bolted down—scraps of paper, balls of dust glommed together with grease from the seat tracks, and an empty cellophane snack bag—swirled behind them before getting caught in the slip-stream and ejected from the opening.

As the plane rose into the dark pre-dawn sky, the jungle canopy became a carpet, variably shaped and colored in a way never apparent from the ground. Even with the adrenalized tunnel vision and terrible focus Jim felt, he still fell into a moment of childlike awe. Marlow banked hard and took them out over the water.

"I'm going to get us offshore so they won't notice us," Marlow said, his voice scratchy over the headset. "Not that they probably would in any event. But we need to surprise them." He flew them far enough to the east that when he finally turned the plane southward, the shore-line was nothing but a thread of beige sand. Jim thought of Jewel down there someplace, and Héctor. The resort staff and guests. The villagers.

This time, he told himself. *This time.*

"Get back into the cargo area. When I give

you the signal, begin dumping the nails. The momentum and kinetics will distribute them over the target. I'll make two passes, so use them accordingly."

Jim unbuckled and crawled between the seats into the cargo hold. For the first time he noticed the rear seats, retracted aft and strapped into the tail. He knelt so he could easily move the nails from their boxes to the door. As a test he stuck his right hand out the howling opening and felt how hard the wind was coming off the wing. He grabbed a hand strap to steady himself.

"I'll get us down to nearly stall speed on the pass," Marlow said. "The drag won't be as bad."

They soon reached the point, just up the beach from Las Posadas, where Marlow intended to make his turn. He banked hard and then turned again, this time aligning with the coastline. Below, the inky surf crashed against the intermittent outcroppings of limestone and coral.

"Almost there," Marlow said over the headset.

Jim had torn the tops off all eight boxes. He had four at his knees ready to drop.

The soft beginnings of dawn provided just enough light for Jim to spot Las Posadas and the ruins below. He could just make out Sherif Ali's men, camouflaged by the darkness, loitering beside the low wall demarcating the beginning of the ruins complex. He didn't know how many were down there, but if they'd filled seven Suburbans, he was guessing it could be upwards of fifty, or if they were lucky, closer to twenty-five or thirty. He was hoping for the latter.

"Hold up," Marlow said. "And hang on."

He banked the plane hard seaward. Jim got jolted hard—backward, he thought thankfully. Righting himself, again he took firm hold of the hand strap.

"We're going to rake that line." Marlow's voice crackled over the earphones. "Then make a turn and do them again from the opposite direction. Be ready."

Jim braced himself with both hands as Marlow took the plane into a precipitous drop in altitude, sending Jim's stomach into his throat. Clearly, Marlow had flown more than just lumbering P-3 Orions in the Navy.

"Ready!" Marlow commanded. "Go!"

Jim dropped the first box of nails, followed by three more in quick succession, out the open hatch. He had no opportunity to see what had happened below before Marlow shot the plane upward.

"Brace yourself," Marlow instructed.

The ballet resumed, churning Jim's stomach in opposing directions once again and then dipping back toward the line of Chevys. Some of Sherif Ali's men looked to the sky while others were sprawled on the ground, and Jim couldn't tell how many were hurt versus just taking cover.

"Ready," came Marlow's order again. "Go!"

Jim dumped the remaining four boxes one by one from the hatch. This time he looked down after the last and saw one man and then another and then a third recoil and stagger before falling to the ground. *Bull's-eye!* he thought triumphantly, but he didn't let his celebration go too far, since he had no idea how many they'd taken fully out of commission.

Just then, he felt something whiz uncomfortably close to his head and realized someone on the ground was shooting and the plane was still in their range.

Marlow must have realized the same. He pulled the plane up as vertical as he could. The wings howled and the engine shuddered, and Jim was thrown back hard against the stowed rear seats and then for a second he floated weightless above the cabin floor before he was tossed against the fuselage, uncomfortably close to the open hatch. *Don't vomit*, he said to himself. *Tighten up.*

Marlow leveled and Jim had a chance to gather himself. His cotton shirt, bleached white by the hardwater pounding Abarrane gave all the wash, was dark with sweat.

"You okay?" Marlow asked over the intercom. "We got 'em. A lot of hits."

Jim touched his ears. Somehow, his headset had remained on. "I'm good," he said. "Copacetic."

"That's my aviator," Marlow said. "We're going to be at the landing point in a moment."

From a crouch, Jim rocked forward and back on his feet, evaluating the give in his huaraches, which were probably not up to the challenge ahead of them. But they'd have to do. Below, the hard ground was closing in.

"Almost there," Marlow said. "You good?"

"I'm good."

"Check on the order of operations?"

"Check," Jim said.

"When we hit the deck, go as soon as it's safe. I'm not going to completely stop rolling. I don't know what's out there."

"Copy," Jim said.

"See you for a beer at sunset."

The plane bounced and settled on the narrow road to the resort, just north of the crossroads. Jim swung his legs out of the hatch. When he felt confident that he could pop and roll, he went, hitting the dirt harder than he would have liked. He heard Marlow's engine spool up, and when he got to his knees, the plane had already taken off, leaving a thick streak of black exhaust trailing behind.

Jim hopped up onto his feet and dusted off his pants, but no sooner than he had begun his run along the hardpack, he heard a terrible groan, the devilish cry of an engine strained beyond its limits. He turned back and saw a heavy wave of black exhaust rolling upward— and then down.

15

As dawn began to soften the dark shadows at the ruins, the billy goat wandered from its preferred shelter near the tower and searched for a nice patch of vetch to munch on. The villagers had come to venerate the goat, associating it with Yum Kaax, the god of wild vegetation and animals. Older than most anyone could remember, the goat was almost as much a part of life in Altún as the ruins themselves.

Which is why it had been no light decision to entrust it with this most important of tasks.

The old goat looked up from its breakfast

when the solemn sound of chanting broke the stillness. Its head turned left, then right, looking for the source. It seemed to be coming from nowhere and everywhere, like the strength of the villagers' beloved San Torcuato.

Across the ruins, on the other side of the fence, Sherif Ali's men were in a state of disarray, some moaning or clutching their shoulders, legs, or arms in agony. Others patted themselves down, feeling for the nails that had rained down and injured their amigos. Their ears were all attuned to the sky, worried the plane would circle back for another strike, when the chanting wafted over on the sea air. They quieted and regrouped, knowing the time had come.

At El Fofo's signal, the twenty-eight men who had survived the strafing without severe injury scrambled over the fence. He led them silently between the two pyramids, through the courtyard, and toward the ball court. From there, the group split into two long snakes and began to encircle the tower and the target on its far side.

El Fofo headed up the line that had rounded the corner of the ball court, and as the chanting got louder, he held up a hand to slow them to a crawl, then pointed left and right to indicate it was time for them to splinter into two groups and close in like a pincer. Ahead, a statue loomed atop the tallest monument, a tower he knew his boss would call "a stupid *pinché* ruin" but that he couldn't help but be impressed by.

As they neared the tower, the field ahead was empty. El Fofo was befuddled. Where were the villagers? Their song couldn't be this loud if they weren't yet at the ruins.

And then he saw it, and he frowned.

The billy goat looked up from the clump of vetch he munched on, seeming to have noted the men's presence. Its tail twitched. Then it popped upward the way goats can, changing direction on the fly, and dashed back toward the tower. A small black rectangle was tied to a rope around its neck, and El Fofo's eyes narrowed as he understood the source of the chanting.

With an animal-like roar, he let loose a stream of bullets that sent the goat on another upward dance, before it crumpled to the grass in a heap. The black box hadn't been hit, and the sound of the villagers continued to reverberate throughout the ruins.

Jim's gait faltered for a moment when he heard the shots.

Thock-thock-thock.

A familiar sense of inadequacy swelled in his chest. Could he do this? Was he good enough? Had he been a lousy soldier? A lousy cop? When it mattered, did he choke?

Was he a coward?

Am I a coward?

He didn't have time to answer himself, as

he'd just reached the edge of the ruins. He saw
the line of Chevys parked along the low north
wall, but not a single Siguiente was visible with
them. He trotted beside one of the step pyramids, the Beretta gripped firmly in his outstretched hands. The villagers' chanting drifted softly through the cool air, and Jim grinned
with the knowledge the enemy had been fooled.

The sun was now peeking up from the edge
of the sea, a mandarin wedge on the horizon.
The old Maya structures cast massive shadows,
and Jim tried to stay hidden as he rounded the
pyramid and neared the nunnery. He dashed
from column to column, but still saw no sign
of Sherif Ali's thugs.

He edged along the north wall of the ball
court, then hopped onto the top ledge to give
himself a vantage point as his own shadow became engulfed by that of the four-tiered tower.

And then he saw them. About thirty men
clad entirely in black were standing in a huge

circle around the slain brown and white goat. El Fofo was in the middle, a tirade of angry words flowing from his mouth as he raised a knee into the air and brought his boot smashing down onto a small black box. It crushed under his heel, and the villagers' prayers finally fell quiet.

In the silence, a series of visions burst through Jim's mind.

Kevin White strode into view, his gun raised and his backpack fat with a bomb. Malinda provided the voice-over. *"It stands for zeolitic imidazolate frameworks. It's space-age solid rocket fuel. Massively explosive."*

Kevin White aimed the muzzle of his assault weapon, trigger drilled to become fully automatic, toward a cowering and weeping group of high school girls.

Thock-thock-thock.

A Black Hawk swooped down onto the

crash pad. The man on Jim's litter stared up at him blankly, the blanket soaked in blood, thick rivers pouring from where limbs should have been. When Jim's gaze returned to the soldier's face, there were only empty sockets where seconds ago his eyes had been.

Thock-thock-thock.

This time the sound wasn't in Jim's head, it had come from his own weapon. His instinct and training had taken over and taken out two Siguientes on the edge of the group. El Fofo's head jerked toward the ball court, but Jim was safely camouflaged in the shadows.

With renewed clarity of mind and purpose, he cradled his pistol, textbook style, and shot another *narco* square between the eyes. He fired down the line of men, like shooting fish in a barrel, hitting a fourth, then a fifth and sixth, before the Siguientes figured out where the gunshots were coming from.

Jim dropped low so the walls of the ball court would protect him from their return fire, and at that moment, he heard whooping and yelling ring out over the ruins.

Yax Pakal's men, armed at least as ferociously as their antagonists, swarmed around the far side of the ball court, catching Sherif Ali's goons by total surprise. San Torcuato peered down approvingly.

Yax Pakal's army was comprised of a group of men every bit as hardened as Sherif Ali's, but they had the ancient blood of Maya warriors. These men served a different god. An angry god.

They advanced at double time without, it appeared, any fear. The *norteños* began falling in bunches. The proverbial tide had turned.

Seeing his men being slaughtered around him, El Fofo beat a retreat to the nunnery. None of his own troops seemed to notice, nor did Yax Pakal's, too embroiled in the fight for territory, for the Balam, but from his vantage atop the ball-court wall, Jim did. With his head down, he rose and raced after Sherif Ali's second, leaving the rest of the Siguientes to their fate with Yax Pakal.

As he neared the edge of the ruins compound, ahead of him El Fofo hurdled the low wall and jumped into the driver's seat of one of the Suburbans. As the engine roared to life, Jim realized El Fofo wasn't alone—Sherif Ali was riding shotgun.

El Fofo threw the truck into reverse and it lurched backward, paused, and then hurtled over the turf toward the beach. Jim fired a single shot, but it pinged off the starboard roof rail as the big black truck went nose-first down into the cover of the dunes. Jim looked out over the ocean. Low tide—they would be able to make it down the beach and toward the village.

Jim slapped the wall in frustration. But it was just two men. There was no way they'd try to take out the entire village themselves, given Yax Pakal's army had just decimated Ali's foot soldiers.

And then it hit Jim. They weren't headed for the village. They were headed for the station house. For Jewel. He needed to get there first.

Jim pivoted on his heel and did a complete one-eighty so he could race back via the path he usually took home from the resort—and came face-to-face with a shirtless man, his chest painted with rivulets of blood, streaming from several puncture wounds.

The *flechettes.*

The man carried an evil-looking machete, its edge bright with careful honing. He lunged and took an upward swing at Jim, who managed to dodge. As the blade flew past his face, he felt a sting just above his right ear. Blood instantly began pouring from the superficial scalp wound, coating the side of Jim's face and spilling down onto his shoulder.

The Siguiente paused at the spectacle and

lowered his machete. He must have thought he hit an artery, Jim figured, and he used that moment of respite to pounce.

Jim raised the Beretta and held it directly to the man's forehead. He fired just as realization was sinking into the man's face, and the man crumpled to the ground with a new rivulet of blood to match his previous wounds.

Knowing he was getting low on ammo, Jim leaned down and prized the machete from the dead man's grip. Then he sprinted off toward the path.

Jim paused for a second at the back gate to the station compound to catch his breath and listen. Nothing. The iron gate hung open. Crouching low, he made his way into the compound. He slunk along the edge of the cannery, but there were no shadows to hide in. He was fully visible from the back side of the veranda, which was empty. He crept around the north side of the house, and at the front corner he squatted low, trying to get a look at the front of the veranda. The deck stood about eye level, and he found himself face-to-face with a pair of dusty boots.

"*Bienvenidos*, Lord Jim," said a husky voice. "You can come out now. But, por favor, hands into the air."

It was Sherif Ali.

Jim dropped the machete and lowered the Beretta carefully to the ground, then raised his hands before walking forward into the hot yard. Sherif Ali sat at the table in Jim's usual chair. El Fofo leaned against the siding of the house, his Sig Sauer resting casually in his grip. On the table, barrel facing in Jim's direction, lay a thick revolver. Jewel sat in the other chair, immobilized and gagged. Her arms were bound to the seat back and her ankles had been tied to the front two legs. Her face was smeared with dirt, but Jim was relieved to see she looked unharmed.

The same could not be said for Héctor, whose limp body Jim saw lying face down on the other side of the front door. His wrists and ankles were bound with the same rope as Jewel's and blood was congealed around a nasty gash on his forehead. He was unconscious, if not worse.

"What do you want?" Jim snarled.

"What do I want? For such a smart guy . . . Jim, we have this conversation before." Sherif Ali spat over the railing. "I thought I make myself clear. But you, you . . ." He paused and shook his head. "You think you are so *pinche* smart. You, gringo, one man"—he held up a single finger—"come here and call himself Lord Jim. You are no lord, my friend. You are one little gringo." He held a cigarette to his lips and lit it, then took a long drag. "You think I will go down so easy? You think I have only these men? You think your *pinche indios* have won?" He shook his head again and made a tsking sound with his tongue. "Is not that easy, amigo." He drew on his cigarette and then flicked it at Jim's feet, before nodding toward El Fofo, who took a step closer behind Jewel.

"For your sins, you son of a whore," he said, and quickly snatched the gun from the table and trained it on Jim. In the same instant, El Fofo raised his gun to Jewel's head.

"I tell you what will be," Sherif Ali continued. "First, you will watch this pretty little whore die for your gringo stupidity. She will be waiting for you in hell, you *chingado, estúpido* gringo." Sherif Ali spat again over the railing at Jim, then glanced over at El Fofo. "Do it," he ordered.

A sinister grin spread across the henchman's face, but it quickly transformed into a pained expression as somehow Jewel, with her coiled, other-worldly energy, managed to flip herself and her chair backward. The top rung of the chairback hooked El Fofo directly below his shiny silver belt buckle and a high-pitched cry escaped his lips as he fell. His gun bounced forward, off the wooden planks of the veranda and down three of the blue steps.

The ruckus momentarily caused Sherif Ali to divert his gaze, and that was all it took.

Jim dove for the steps and scooped up the Sig Sauer in one swift action, and sunk a round square in Sherif Ali's mustachioed face. The Siguientes jefe clattered backward onto the worn treads of the veranda, falling into the mess of his own spattered brains.

El Fofo tried impotently to free himself from Jewel and the chair, his face contorted with panic and severe pain. He patted around himself for his gun, not realizing it was his own weapon that had just assassinated his boss.

Jim stepped onto the veranda and unhooked Jewel's chair from El Fofo's belt buckle, letting him fall to the floor, then whispered in her ear as he brought her upright. "That was incredible. You're going to be okay." He kissed her forehead, and then her lips, aware that to the side El Fofo was climbing with some effort to his hands and knees. As the man began trying to crawl away, Jim kicked him in the ribs and he fell back down.

El Fofo inched away in a scooting crab walk, blubbering and begging for mercy. "Por favor, Señor Lord. Por favor."

Jim took mercy in the only way he could: with a shot straight to the heart that killed El Fofo instantly.

He moved over to Héctor, rolling his friend onto his back. A gasp crossed the older man's lips and Jim could see the rise and fall of his chest as his eyes began to flutter open.

"*Qué pasó?*" he asked weakly, and Jim shushed him.

"Amigo, you're okay now. Everything's okay."

He grabbed the dive knife from Héctor's holster and returned to Jewel, cutting loose the bindings that held her to the chair. He pulled her up and she collapsed into his arms. Their hearts beat against each other's chests in frantic, opposing rhythms, until they began to slow and sync, finding steadiness in unison. He'd never held her that close before and he was suddenly overcome with emotion. Love, for the amazing woman he'd thought he was going to lose; pride, for having come out on top when the odds were towering against him; sorrow, for how bloody that day had had to become.

And redemption. Because this time he hadn't choked. He wasn't a coward. He had been a soldier along with the villagers and protected Jewel and did what needed to be done.

He laughed, even as tears flowed down his cheeks. Curious, Jewel pulled away and got a good look at Jim for the first time that morning.

"What happened? So much blood. Let me see."

Jim had forgotten all about his head wound, and tilted so she could look at the long cut above his ear.

She gasped.

"I'll live," he said. "It's long, but it isn't deep."

"I don't know about that, tough guy." She went into the house and returned with a small towel from the kitchen, which she pressed firmly against Jim's head.

Just then, the white Posadas Land Cruiser that Jim and Marlow had driven to the airstrip before dawn pulled into the yard, kicking up a rooster tail of dust halfway back to the crossroads. It skidded to a stop in front of the house, and Marlow jumped out.

His face was a mess. Tracks of sweat and blood ran across the dirt and soot caked on his cheeks. Strips torn from what had once been his fight jacket were tied around his forehead, soaked through with blood. As he descended from the Toyota, Jim detected a limp in his right leg.

"You look like hell," Marlow said to Jim.

"I was going to say the same."

"There was a little drama just after I dropped you. No biggie."

"What happened?"

"Maybe one of those shots from the ground might have hit."

"*Might* have hit?"

"It's the jungle, Jim. There's gremlins everywhere. What the hell happened to you?"

"This?" Jim gingerly lifted the wad of cloth from the gash to show Marlow.

"No, no, no," Jewel said, guiding his hand back to the wound, which still oozed blood.

"One of the guys we hit with the flechettes wasn't very happy," Jim said. "I had to explain that it wasn't personal, just business."

"Business," Marlow said ruefully with a slow shake of his head. "Bloodiest business there is. What's the forensics on this?" He pointed past Jim and Jewel. "The storm behind you."

The bodies of Sherif Ali and El Fofo lay askew,

their blood dripping through the planks to the limestone below.

"Forty-five caliber shots to the head and chest, respectively," Jim said. "Single weapon." Jim handed El Fofo's Sig Sauer over to Marlow. "This was found at the scene."

Marlow took the gun and slid it into the back of his waistband. As he did, a flash of movement from the left caught his attention as Héctor managed to pull himself into a seated position and rested against the wall of the house.

"Don Carlos," he said to Marlow with a weak smile. "You made it."

"At a price," Marlow said, striding over and kneeling before his friend. "To you, as well. I guess I was wrong that they wouldn't come through here."

"The big one caught me by surprise and clocked me good. I don't know how long I was out. It's lucky Señor Lord came along when he did."

"Lucky indeed. Are you okay besides that major goose egg?"

"I think so."

"Good man, good man." Marlow squeezed Héctor's shoulder, then rose and returned to Jim.

"Let me have a look at that," he said to Jewel, who was still tending to Jim's gash. She gently removed the now-saturated wad of cloth. "You're not going to like this, Jim, but that needs a suture."

"I don't even like the sound of it."

Jewel went into the house and returned with fresh cotton towels, a needle from her sewing kit, a bottle of tequila, and a spool of forty-pound line she had found in a rarely used tackle box Cornelius had forgotten in the storage room.

Marlow set to work.

"Not bad until the end," Jim said when he was done, reapplying pressure to the now-sewn wound. In truth, it had hurt like mad. He didn't know whether Marlow's clumsy needle pricks or the rough way he pulled the fishing line through his skin hurt more.

Jewel, who had seen the anguish in Jim's expression with each stitch, took his face in her hands and kissed his forehead.

"It will stop the bleeding at least," Marlow said. "Most of it. Any concussion?"

"No, it was pretty glancing. What about you?"

"Me?" Marlow said. "I'm still seeing double."

That explained a lot, Jim thought.

Suddenly Héctor piped up, his voice sounding almost strong again. "Look at the water. There's zodiacs coming in from a cutter out there. Feds be here any second. You should go. Pronto."

"But I'm done running," Jim protested.

"Listen to Héctor, Jim," Marlow said. "It was one thing to stand up to the Siguientes. But sticking around when the *Federales* come to clean up the mess is just stupid. You and I need to get out of here, now."

"Not without Jewel," Jim said, clutching her hand.

"Of course Jewel's coming. I'm not blind. Go in and gather some of your things, enough to last a few days, at least. And anything of value, lest it find its way into a Fed's pocket."

While Jewel and Jim hurriedly packed, Marlow sank down next to Héctor. "You going to be okay, amigo?"

"I just tell the truth, right, jefe?" He rose with Marlow's help. "I was minding my own business when all of a sudden I was knocked out on the porch. When I came to, there were two dead bodies and a whole lot of blood. I didn't hear nothing, didn't see no one. Ghosts."

"You didn't need any more ghosts, Héctor," Marlow said softly.

Jim rushed out the front door lugging his duffel, with Jewel right behind carrying a smaller bag. They dashed down the steps and Jim tossed the bags into the back of the Toyota.

He looked at Héctor and nodded in farewell. "Gracias, Héctor . . . for everything."

"*Batab* Jim, you stay in touch," he called to Jim as he shuffled toward a chair and sank into it. "And you, old man," he said to Marlow, who was crawling behind the wheel of the truck, "not so much. Always so much trouble wherever you go."

Marlow's airplane sat on the apron of the airstrip at Xcalak. The undercarriage had been scorched black.

"What the hell happened, Chuck?" Jim asked.

"I might have misjudged the envelope a little after dropping you off," Marlow said.

"A little?"

"Maybe a lot. But I got it sorted. In time."

"It can fly?"

"All you need is a propeller and a pair of

wings. You ever see the Wright Flyer at the Air and Space Museum?"

"What about the avionics?"

"The sort of flying we'll be doing? It doesn't use a lot of avionics."

"No avionics?"

"We will be, literally, under the radar."

Jim helped Marlow wrestle the cargo door out of the hold and back into its hinges. Marlow shot and locked it and did his preflight walkaround. For as rough as he had been treating the plane, it still looked nice and tight.

"Where are we going?" Jim asked.

"Good question. Anywhere in Mexico is probably too hot for us. I'm not sure the States is a good idea, either. I still have some contacts in Panama City. Old-timers and old friends. It's not what it used to be, but a person can still disappear down there for a time to cool off. I haven't flown it for a long time, but I think I remember a few backdoors in along the west coast near the canal. We could slip in easy enough."

"What about Tamarindo?" Jewel said, surprising both men.

"Tamarindo, Costa Rica?" Marlow asked.

"Yes."

"I've been in and out of Nosara a few times," Marlow said, thoughtfully inspecting one of the air-speed pitot tubes. "Why on earth Tamarindo?"

Jim looked at Jewel quizzically as well.

"I know someone there. Sort of a fairy godmother. She always said if things got too . . . 'busy,' I think was her word, I could visit her in Tamarindo. I hear it's quite pretty."

"This time of year," Jim joked.

"Always," she said, giving him a playful nudge with her shoulder.

"What's this fairy godmother's name?" Marlow asked.

"Rosemary Page. I've known her all my life."

"Do you think she has room for a couple of other orphans?" Jim asked.

"I think so," she said. "She's very generous."

"That'll do," Marlow said, and with a bow and flourish, he gestured toward the cockpit. "All aboard the Tamarindo Express."

Jewel gave the taxi driver the address after he'd stowed their bags in the trunk, and a slight flicker of interest crossed his eyes when he heard the street name. He drove them up the coast and then turned a bit inland, taking a winding road through the low hills above Tamarindo Bay.

He dropped them off outside a grand Spanish Colonial–style house, surrounded by a wall draped in blooming bougainvillea. Tall palms rustled in a slight wind.

When Jewel rang the bell, a short, dark woman in a colorful floral frock opened the door.

Her eyes grew wide when she saw Jewel and a grin overtook her stern features. "*Mi querida!*" she exclaimed. "*Pasen, pasen!*"

She waved her arms to gesture them inside, then waddled off, leaving them in a formal dining room. The heavy table was surrounded by remarkably fine colonial mahogany furniture. A santo perched in a niche in a wall above a priceless seventeenth-century colonial buffet. Outside, there was a colonnaded porch, and at the center, a pristine white pool surrounded by grass.

"The architecture and furnishings," Marlow muttered to himself, "it's the strangest coincidence . . ."

Before Jim could ask what he meant, an elegant woman wearing a white floor-length shift in the native style entered from a door opposite the one they had entered.

"Rosemary!" Jewel cried, and she rushed into the older woman's arms, allowing her tears to finally flow, her narrow shoulders shuddering in relief. Rosemary's arms wrapped around her protectively, and she cooed soothingly into Jewel's ear.

When they broke their embrace, Jewel returned to Jim's side and linked her arm through his.

"This is Jim Lord," she said, "the man I've written to you about."

"Ah, yes, Señor Lord," Rosemary said, offering her hand to Jim, who shook it politely. "Thank you for all you have done for Jewel. You are most welcome in my home."

Then she turned her gaze to Chuck Marlow. "Mr. Marlow, I presume," she said, extending a hand. "I'm charmed, after all these years."

Marlow looked at her quizzically, and she raised an eyebrow in return, then tipped her head toward a series of framed photographs on the buffet. Marlow perused the faces, which included a teenage Jewel, and smiled when he got to an image of a dark-haired man with a pointy chin and bushy mustache. The man's round glasses didn't hide the kindness in his eyes, which seemed to twinkle even in sepia tones.

Marlow murmured, "I knew this house reminded me of someone. I should have known the moment I saw the furniture, especially this buffet."

"Who?" Jim blurted, completely befuddled as to what was going on. "Do you two already know each other?"

Rosemary laughed. "Not each other, but we have a good friend in common."

"Javier Klopp, it would seem," Marlow said, giving Rosemary a conspiratorial grin. From the moment he'd walked in, the house had felt familiar. Indeed, the rich colonial antiques reminded him of nothing, or no one person, so much as Javier Klopp. Marlow had only been to Klopp's house in Polanco once, but his extensive collection of colonial furniture had left a lasting impression.

Marlow's eyes shifted to Jewel and he let them linger on her features a moment before glancing back and forth between the young woman and the photo of the mustached man. Then his expression shifted from surprise to understanding. "So she is . . ." He trailed off, looking to Rosemary for confirmation.

Rosemary nodded. "It's time she knew, anyway." She held out a hand to summon Jewel, who gripped it tightly and let herself be led to the sitting room. Jim and Marlow followed, each taking a chair while Rosemary and Jewel settled on the couch in between.

"What's going on?" Jewel asked, her innocent tone making her seem almost a child again.

"My dear girl," Rosemary said, "I always told you that one day the time would be right for you to learn about your father. I think this is that time. Your father is Javier Klopp. I was his first employee." There was a fond remembrance in her tone. "I served as bookkeeper and office manager for this fresh little company on Front Street in Belize City, started by Javier right after graduating from UNAM." She smiled and paused for a minute, clearly enjoying her memory of the man. Then her expression turned a little dark.

"After a year, a British Honduran began working for him. In those days, before independence, the country was a mixed bag of colonials, most with British backgrounds muddled by many years of living in the dangerous business of mahogany export. The man's name was Cornelius O'Connor and he'd made his mark learning the names of all the men who needed bribing in Belize City. Under mysterious circumstances, he had married the daughter of a mahogany plantation owner. It was not a love match. Cornelius O'Connor had his eyes on one day inheriting the plantation."

Jim groaned. That sounded exactly like Cornelius, all right.

"O'Connor brought his beautiful bride, Jaylin Vasquez, to Belize City," Rosemary continued, "which is where his employer, the young and handsome Javier Klopp, fell in love. Their attraction was instantaneous and undeniable, and Jaylin told Javier she'd been forced to marry and did not love her husband.

"Shortly after Jaylin's arrival, the poor girl's parents turned up dead. At nearly the exact same time, Cornelius O'Connor was apprehended on the twin charges of extortion of public officials, as he had been double accounting, and pederasty, still a crime in the Empire. Javier got him smuggled safely out of the country and up to a palm plantation he owned in Mexico. O'Connor, ever imperious, insisted his wife be sent after him. Javier agreed, intending it to only be temporary, until he could pull some strings and get her marriage annulled. He hadn't known her condition when she left." Rosemary twisted her hands in her lap and let out a wistful sigh.

"And then she died. Javier was beside himself, but there was nothing he could do. He couldn't admit to having fathered a child out of wedlock, and he'd confided in nobody but me, so his parents had no idea. They arranged for him to be engaged to the beautiful and wealthy daughter of a magistrate of the Mexican Supreme Court. And so he was. He went on to have a large family of his own, but he never stopped thinking about you."

Rosemary let out a rueful sigh, then gripped Jewel's fingers with her own and gazed deep into the young woman's eyes. "I'm so sorry that you had to grow up under the malevolent watch of Cornelius O'Connor. But we knew you also had Abarrane and the wonderful women of

Altún to raise you. And I hope you knew I was always there for you as well."

Tears glided down Jewel's cheeks, and she squeezed Rosemary's hands, nodding.

"Javier asked me to keep a refuge for you, should you ever need to be spirited away," Rosemary continued. "When I retired, he bought me this home as a thank you for my long years of devoted service, but also to be a safe house for you, if and when you needed it. While I hoped for your sake that day would never come, you will always be welcome in this home. In our home. And your friends will always be welcome, too."

Jewel stayed silent, but her head slid down onto Rosemary's shoulder. The older woman stroked her hair, temple to neck, over and over. The soothing motion soon put Jewel to sleep.

* * *

A shower rejuvenated Jim considerably, finally washing away the dirt and sweat and blood
from Altún. If only it could have washed away
the death and destruction as well—but at least
this time Jim wouldn't be plagued by cowardice and failure. No, this time he had stood his
ground and helped save an entire village. Saved
the woman he loved.

Downstairs, he found Jewel and Marlow,
both freshly bathed as well, sitting at the dining
table with Rosemary Page, a delicious spread
awaiting. As the four of them enjoyed a salad of
brilliantly colored fruits, ceviche, and tamales,
Jim felt at peace. Whatever aftershocks might
come from the carnage of Altún, he and Jewel
would be safe. Rosemary clearly regarded Jewel
with the ferocity of a mother and seemed to be
embracing him as a son. Jim even wondered if

he might have noticed a little spark between her and Marlow.

After the *cena*, Marlow pulled Jim aside. "I have to go, Jim. I can't stay. Not now. There's places I need to be."

"Not even for the night?" Jim asked.

Marlow shook his head. "It's better if I don't. Costa Rican air force no doubt captured the transponder signal on my plane coming in. Just to be safe, I better make myself scarce."

"No, Chuck, no way. We're in this together. I'm not letting you take the fall for what happened up there."

"Don't worry about me, Jim. Remember what I told you? The Mexicans will figure out a way to spin it. If your name comes up, which it won't, they'll name you as a casualty."

"How can you be so sure it won't?"

"Because you're in love with the natural daughter of one of the richest men in the world.

And she credits you with saving her life. She's also more than a little in love with you, in case you haven't noticed."

Jim blushed, abashed, unable to hide his sappy smile.

"You've been reborn, Jim. You grew into yourself and have a second chance at life. Not many are so lucky." Chuck glanced toward the dining room, where Rosemary still sat at the table. "I have no use here anymore, though I'll be back. I think Señora Page and I need to get better acquainted. But that's another story." He grasped Jim's shoulder and squeezed.

"You really think I've proved myself?" Jim's confident tone belied that even he knew the answer to his question.

"I certainly do. *Batab* Jim."

Other books by
KERRY McDONALD

Into Africa
In a world ruled by British colonialism,
when her missionary brother appeals for her
help, Janet Livingstone must confront her
deep prejudice and organize a rescue mission
to Africa. A woman's take on the story of
Stanley and Livingstone.

The Green Cathedral
In this sweeping, sci-fi love story, a corrupt
DEA agent, on the run from past mistakes,
discovers a dangerous alien woman living in
the jungle. He must sacrifice everything to
help her return to her planet.

Stay up to date:

Follow Kerry on Amazon & Goodreads

https://www.amazon.com/author/
mcdonaldkerry